I SHALL NOT MATE

Neil Riebe

I Shall Not Mate
Copyright © 2017 by Neil Riebe
Illustrations © 2018 Neil Riebe
Cover design © 2018 Neil Riebe

ISBN: 978-1-7944-8246-3

For Cody Bratsch, Zach Cole, Breyden Halverson, Christofer Nigro, and the rest of the Attack of the Kaiju *gang. Your enthusiasm encouraged me to make this story grander than its original premise.*

Part 1

1

Forty years ago, volcanic action raised up an island in the South Pacific, long after the waters had been charted. It lay in the sun, far from the sea lanes used by merchant ships. It escaped human eyes, but it did not escape the eyes of the pterosaurs called the Flock.

They descended upon an escarpment overlooking the coast. The escarpment buckled under their weight. Dust puffed up around their feet and loose rock tumbled down the slope. Flaking Scales was their matriarch. She was the tallest of the group, standing sixty-two meters in height, and had a wingspan of a hundred forty-five meters. Past her breeding years, she croaked to her fellow pterosaurs, expressing her satisfaction with the island. It is a good place, she assured them. The ground was firm. It was high above the waves, safe from storms and seaborne predators.

Her companions included three fifty-meter tall breeding age adults—two of them were female and one was a male—and two three-meter tall juveniles who were sisters. They clucked with enthusiasm amongst each other. They trusted the ancient matriarch. Even though her eyesight was fading, she had seen more of the world than they had and understood the mysteries of the seasons and the tides, the ways of the winds, the clouds, and the rain.

Flaking Scales called the three Flock members of breeding age. They shuffled to her on all fours, forming a circle. In a series of clucks and croaks, Flaking Scales told them that this was the time to lay eggs.

The more of us there are the wiser we shall become, she croaked.

We can never be as wise as you, Yellow Claws replied. She was one of the females of breeding age. The scales on her fingers were a bright yellow.

Flaking Scales rubbed her beak against Yellow Claws' to show her appreciation.

Go, she clucked. *Pick a place to nest. Lay your eggs.*

Yellow Claws and White Sail, who was the other breeding age female, glided over the island, searching for an ideal place to lay their eggs. White Sail picked a spot which was situated at the bottom of a hill. She was called White Sail because the sail atop her head was all white with no color banding. Yellow Claws had little imagination, and chose to dig her nest at the foot of the same hill.

Their nesting sites chosen, they called out to the breeding age male. To his chagrin, they called him Male. He wanted to be recognized as Rainbow Sail, because his sail had the brightest color bands. They made him look fetching. But the Flock named its members based on an individual's most distinctive characteristic. Since he was the only male, being male was his most distinctive characteristic. Hence he was stuck with a bland name.

He circled over them, answering their calls with calls of his own and then dropped down between them. Male displayed his sail to the fullest as if to remind them he should be recognized by that rather than his sex before folding it down atop his head.

Yellow Claws and White Sail stretched their sails out to the fullest to show they welcomed his companionship.

Flaking Scales led the two juveniles out to sea in search of food. Filling their bellies would keep the juveniles occupied so the breeding age members of the Flock could have their privacy. When she returned, Flaking Scales found that Male had chosen White Sail. Yellow Claws sat in her empty nest with the stigma of rejection hanging heavy over her.

Flaking Scales landed beside her and clucked, reminding her that she will be able to fill her nest next season.

Only because I am the only female left, Yellow Claws grumbled. *Not because I am wanted.*

Yellow Claws' sorrow reminded Flaking Scales of her youth, when it was easy to become discouraged and jealous. Now that youthful passions no longer fired her blood, she could see mating's pragmatic purpose. It did not matter if you were chosen first, second, or third. What mattered was that you contributed to the growth of the Flock. Yellow Claws was too young to understand.

After a full cycle of the moon had passed, White Sail filled her nest with five eggs. She and Male swelled with pride. No other pairing had produced so many eggs. The most anyone had laid was three. Well, according to them.

Flaking Scales chuckled in a warbling croak. *I have seen nests filled with six eggs*, she clucked.

The others gathered around her to hear more, except for White Sail, who protectively sat upon her eggs with her wings splayed over the nest like blankets.

Flaking Scales had nothing else to add, except: *It does not matter how many eggs you lay. What matters is how many of your chicks survive onto adulthood. Guard your chicks. Teach them to fight or the predators will eat them and the humans will kill them. Beware of disease. It is a silent killer. Keep the chicks warm, fed, and be sure they sleep. Most of all beware of the Two-Headed One.*

The Flock bowed their heads in remembrance of the Two-Headed One. They originally came from a colony of five Flocks. The Two-Headed One, called Tiamatodon by the humans, wiped out their colony and set their former island home ablaze. Flaking Scales was the sole survivor of her Flock. She rallied Yellow Claws, White Sail, Male and the two juveniles to form a new Flock. They flew south to escape Tiamatodon.

The Two-Headed One does not eat meat, Flaking Scales croaked. *The Two-Headed One does not eat the green things that sprout from the soil. It lives on Death itself.*

White Sail left the nest under Male's care and flew to the palm grove on the coast. She plucked several trees bare of their fronds and put the fronds in a pile. For a moment she paused to scan the ocean. The endless waves appeared to be as barren as the dunes out in the desert. A cloud bank stretched across the horizon. Sunlight brought out the white magnificence of its summit. However, the cloudbank had a dark underbelly.

What was that?

Did she see lightning?

White Sail stiffened, becoming as motionless as the stones. Her white fur fluttered in the breeze.

It was a day like this when the Flock seemed safe that the Two-Headed One rose up out of the sea. First the sky turned black. Thunder boomed in her ears. The wind howled, whipping rain into her face. And then the harbinger of destruction came up onto the shore. White Sail was a giant in the animal kingdom, standing taller than the elephants and the giraffes. She stood taller than many of the world's trees. The Two-Headed One dwarfed her. It dwarfed Flaking Scales. It was the tallest thing she had ever seen walk the Earth.

The sharp keel that stuck out of her chest was firm enough to crack bones. All of her Flock mates had one. They struck the Two-Headed One over and over. Their keels scratched its tough hide but did not draw blood. Nothing stopped it. Nothing. It drew lightning out of the sky and spewed its energy from its two mouths, setting fire to the rookeries and blasted the matriarchs from the air. The fire. The black smoke. That deafening double roar. She never wanted to go through such a nightmare again.

White Sail looked in one direction and then another. There was nothing out there. Just waves. No lightning. No harbinger of destruction. Just memories.

She picked up the palm fronds and flew back to the nest.

Male greeted her with a friendly chittering sound.

White Sail dropped the foliage and acknowledged him with a long throaty cluck.

The five eggs were a creamy yellow with orange spots. They lay in a shallow pit White Sail had dug into the warm black sand. She turned them over with her beak to be sure they were not cracked, pausing often to admire them. She then pulled out the old fronds from the bottom of the nest and replaced them with the fresh ones, rolling the eggs out of the way so the fronds could be placed.

White Sail felt Flaking Scales' critical eye on her back. She could sense that the old matriarch thought that she was working harder than necessary. White Sail continued lining the bottom of the nest anyway. Doting over her eggs made her feel like she was being a good mother.

Once finished, she hunkered down among her eggs, drawing her wings over the nest to keep it warm. White Sail nodded off to sleep. There she sat, hunched over the nest, breathing slowly. While she dreamt of her future offspring becoming masters of the sky, the eggs began to stir. White Sail opened one eye. When she felt an egg pop open, she became fully awake. Hopping off the nest, she called the others to gather around to watch the newborns hatch.

Despite her jealousy, Yellow Claws became as excited as White Sail. Flaking Scales watched without uttering so much as a single cluck. The hive mind of the Flock allowed White Sail and her Flock mates to be aware of the old matriarch's feelings. She saw this hatching as the rebirth of the Flock and the first step toward rebuilding the Flock colony that had been destroyed by the Two-Headed One.

The first hatchling spread her wings in an attempt to burst her egg all the way open. As she exerted herself to the fullest she let out a shrill peep, which sounded adorable to the adult females. However, the membrane inside the egg held the broken shell together.

A second hatchling chewed her way out of her egg and tumbled onto the palm fronds lining the nest. She was tiny, about the size of an adult human, and sticky with embryonic fluid.

The third and fourth eggs wobbled as the hatchlings inside struggled to break free.

The fifth egg so far remained still.

Concerned, White Sail nudged it with her beak.

Flaking Scales hissed at her to leave it alone. Be patient.

The two juveniles glided overhead. They were unimpressed.

The hatchlings will never be as strong as us, they confided to each other in soft clucks and in a warbling chorus sang out, *Human fodder! Human fodder!*

White Sail dismissed their comments. When they reached breeding age they would understand how precious hatchlings were.

It was just as well the juveniles remained in the air. They spotted a predator coming ashore. The juveniles screeched in alarm.

The adults hushed and listened. Their sails popped up atop their heads when they heard the thump of footsteps coming inland. Flaking Scales rallied everyone into the air.

White Sail refused. Her clutch would be defenseless. She climbed into her nest and hid her hatchlings under her wings.

Flaking Scales dropped back down onto the ground and head-butted White Sail out of the nest. She hissed savagely at the young mother.

White Sail snapped out of her panic and joined the rest of the Flock. Pterosaurs held the advantage fighting from the air, not the ground.

Down on the beach, Tylogon, the kaiju *Tylosaurus*, was crawling on his belly toward the ridge. In the sea he was agile, but on land he struggled like a worm. He was seven times longer than the largest whales. He hunted in the deep ocean trenches, but he must had caught the Flock's scent when he came up for air. To be more specific, he must had smelled the calorie-rich embryonic juices coming from the eggs.

Flaking Scales dove with her wings outstretched and her beak held high, coming in at Tylogon's flank. She aimed to sever his spine. The keratin covering her chest keel caught the sun, giving it the shine of a hatchet blade. As she neared her target, Tylogon raised his dorsal fin. The spines supporting the fin were sharp and as hard as iron. Flaking Scales could still strike Tylogon's spine but in return the spines would pierce her belly. The matriarch cut her run short before she impaled herself.

Yellow Claws circled overhead, trying to pick an angle of attack. The dorsal fin ran the entire length of his back. So, she targeted his head, coming down low, skimming the earth. Her slipstream left a cloud of black sand in her wake.

Tylogon triggered his belly to convulse. As she came within range, he spewed a glob of stomach juice, splashing Yellow Claws on the right shoulder and face. She screeched. The impact of the corrosive liquid broke her flight run. She tumbled in the sand and rolled past him and into the water.

The sea lizard roared. His call shocked the shore with its reverberation. However, it was not a cry of rage but of joy. White Sail could see this was a game to him. He was confident that he would return to the sea with a full belly. She circled the shore, trying to think of a way to get around that fin.

The two juveniles landed on his back, hooked their claws into his scales, and nipped at his flesh.

Tylogon coiled around, faster than expected. His jaws made a loud crack as they snapped shut and just missed seizing one of the juveniles.

The small pterosaurs cawed in amusement. They flew in and out of his reach to see if they could rile him.

Yellow Claws fluttered like a wounded butterfly, trying to gain altitude. Smoke puffed from her wounds as the stomach acid dissolved her flesh.

Male dove for Tylogon's tail, coming low across the beach. The dust trail his slipstream left behind drew Tylogon's attention. He struck Male with his tail before Male could strike with his chest keel. The blow hurled Male toward the shoreline along with a fine spray of water that flung from Tylogon's massive rear appendage. The male pterosaur kicked up chunks of moist sand as he rolled to a stop. He shook his head to regain his senses. Struggling to get back up on all fours, he took a couple of unsteady steps and collapsed.

Tylogon scaled the ridge. He paused at the summit to find the source of the smell of fresh eggs. Spotting the nest a thousand meters inland, he lumbered forward. His flanks swung side to side as his webbed paws sank into the ground, leaving a trail of deep footprints. The sight of prey put a twinkle in his eyes.

By this time a third egg had hatched. Three hatchlings now lay helpless.

Out of desperation White Sail dropped down before Tylogon, blocking his path. She hissed ferociously and then snapped her beak at him.

Tylogon jerked back to avoid getting bit and then lunged forward, grabbing White Sail in his jaws. He shocked her with bolts of electricity. White Sail's bones rattled in her body as electric arcs snapped from the sea monster's mouth. He shook her until she was senseless then cast her aside and closed on the nest. Flaking Scales buzzed him to frighten him away. He flashed his open jaws at her in warning to not get too close or else she too would feel his electrified bite.

Because the hatchlings were not her own, Flaking Scales could not bring herself to risk her life for them.

White Sail lay like a broken kite.

The nest was defenseless.

Tylogon's shadow fell upon the hatchlings.

The three hatchlings peeped for help.

No help was coming.

The second hatchling, the one that had chewed its way out of its egg, bit the webbing between Tylogon's toes, slicing through the thick skin.

Tylogon snapped his paw away before she could take a second bite. The hatchling fluttered up and took a nick out of his snout. White Sail's beak opened in surprise when she saw her newborn cut through the hard scales. Tylogon hissed, flashing his teeth to frighten the hatchling. Instead of flying away, the hatchling saw opportunity. She fluttered inside the mouth and sliced off the tip of Tylogon's tongue. The pink tip of flesh bounced once inside the nest and rolled amongst the other two hatchlings. They paused in their pleas for help to eat the tiny morsel.

Tyolgon shut his mouth and backed up from the nest with the ferocious hatchling flapping feverishly to keep up with his retreat.

By then Male had regained his senses and rejoined Flaking Scales. They attacked at the same time, diving from opposite directions. The matriarch's keel made a meaty sound as it impacted Tylogon's brow while Male made a second attempt at the tail, leaving a red gouge in the thick meat. Drops of blood rained down onto the hard soil from the wounds.

Fed up, Tylogon wriggled back to the ridge, slid down its slope, and returned to the sea. The Flock glided overhead, screeching at him to never make landfall on their island again.

The second hatchling fluttered back to the nest after Tylogon swam back into the sea. She hissed at her siblings to be quiet. The danger was over. Seeing that the first hatchling was still struggling to get out of its egg, the second hatchling wrenched the loose piece of eggshell free. The first hatchling rolled out and bumped her head on the bottom of the nest. Disoriented, she blinked and then resumed peeping in distress.

The adults gathered around. White Sail inspected her injuries and found the bite marks to be superficial. It appeared that Tylogon wanted dessert first. Carnivores, and most omnivores, considered eggs to be a delicacy.

Yellow Claws' face had been disfigured by the acid attack. However, the burns had no effect on her fertility, so she was confident that her desirability had not been reduced. The burns did itch. Flaking Scales nipped her whenever she tried to scratch them. Scratching could make the wound susceptible to infection.

White Sail observed that the third hatchling was a male. This was good. Males were rare, and with two more eggs to go her clutch might reveal a second.

While they waited, Flaking Scales urged the adults to name the three newborns that had already hatched.

White Sail touched the second hatchling with the tip of her beak and chittered, *Razor Beak. I have never seen anyone with such a powerful bite.*

The others reflected on how the second hatchling cut the skin to a beast a hundred times her size. Not even human weapons had punctured Tylogon's tough hide. They nodded, chittering in agreement. The second hatchling was to be known as Razor Beak.

White Sail touched the first hatchling and called her Peeps.

The others found the name fitting.

As for the newborn male, he had no distinguishing characteristics except for the fact he was a male and the Flock already had a member called "Male".

Male suggested that the newborn go by "Male" and he be called "Rainbow Sail". He extended his sail to remind the females of its brilliant color bands.

Flaking Scales snorted in disapproval. The matter was dropped.

White Sail couldn't think of a name. For the time being the newborn would be nameless.

The fourth egg cracked open. All eyes turned, watched, and waited. The hatchling kicked the shell in half. White Sail and the other adults drew in their breath. The hatchling fell backward into the larger of the two pieces of egg shell and rolled over before anyone could get a good look at it. It laid underneath the shell, quivering.

Impatient to see if she got another male, White Sail bent down to remove the shell. Flaking Scales batted White Sail's beak with her own. The young mother was cowed into waiting under the senior female's harsh glare.

Newborns must not be helped. Hatching was the first test of their strength.

Eventually, the fourth hatchling crawled out from underneath its shell. It turned out to be another female.

White Sail invested her hope in the fifth egg. It continued to lie still. She feared that it might be a stillborn.

To encourage the young mother to get her mind off the fifth egg, Flaking Scales nudged White Sail to name the fourth hatchling.

White Sail found her to be as unremarkable as the newborn male. She shook her head, indicating she could not think of a name. Neither could any of the others.

Being given a name afforded a Flock pterosaur a degree of distinction that an unnamed Flock member would have to earn by accomplishing a useful feat such as locating nesting ground, finding food, or fending off predators. Most Flock pterosaurs had no names. The two juveniles were examples. They had no distinguishing characteristics and accomplished nothing important.

Names also helped attract the fittest mates, provided the name demanded respect, like Razor Beak. "Peeps" would probably turn away mates, unless the first hatchling could get it changed by accomplishing an important feat. Judging by her behavior, that did not look likely.

The four hatchlings looked up at the adults inquisitively. They figured out by instinct who their parents were and stared at White Sail and Male, wanting attention. Their parents were too focused on the fifth egg to give them any. The hatchlings gave up trying to interact with the adults and gazed with listless eyes at their surroundings.

The last egg wobbled.

White Sail breathed easy in relief.

It remained still for another moment then a wing punched through the shell. The adults hissed in shock. The wing was brown. Stillborns were known to turn brown as they rotted inside the egg. This hatchling had the same death color, yet it lived. And the hand had an extra digit—an opposable thumb. To the Flock this was not a miracle. It was a grotesquery. The delicate fingers scratched the outside of the egg with its claws. The sound set White Sail's beak on edge. A fine dust of pulverized calcium wafted from the claw marks. The thing inside the egg let out a screech. It was unnaturally loud and hideous. White Sail could only image what this creature was going to look like once it hatched.

2

The fifth hatchling enjoyed a life of warmth and darkness. His world seemed boundless as he floated inside his capsule of embryonic fluid, until he outgrew his egg. His boundless universe turned claustrophobic. The pain in his cramped limbs signaled to him he had better get out, quickly. His feeble legs kicked at the shell to no avail. He squirmed about. His anxiety intensified until out of reflex he punched the side of his prison.

A sharp crack sounded in his ears. At least to his ears the sound seemed sharp. It was actually quite subtle, but it was the loudest noise he had heard in his insular existence.

The alien scent of the outside world leaked into the egg. He summoned his strength and punched once more. This time his wing smashed through the concave wall and out into a cooler realm. He grasped the outside of the shell in an effort to pull himself out. His claws slid down the egg's surface and when his wing lowered, a shaft of light pierced the hole and stung his eyes. He let out a sharp screech.

He rested a moment to acclimate himself to his new reality and then finished the job of hatching from his egg. Around him were four other hatchlings. They regarded him with empty stares. One peeped incessantly. Two others pecked at a piece of pink meat, tearing bits off and swallowing them down their slender necks.

The piece of meat stirred his appetite. Before he could wobble over to get a bite for himself he heard a commotion overhead. Looking up he saw four giants that looked much like his siblings, all white with russet colored beaks and claws. One had yellow fingers and red sores on its face. Another had deep wrinkles in its neck. There were scales hanging loose from its face and limbs. A third was distressed while the fourth remained calm, muttering in response to the cawing of the other three.

His instinct identified which of the four giants were his parents. He felt a special connection with his mother. He had sensed her warmth and affection when she roosted on the nest.

However, she no longer had any affection for him. She squawked in horror at what he turned out to be.

The fifth hatchling didn't understand what was wrong, yet he felt ashamed because his body upset the adults. The scales were brown and the fur on his torso was black, instead of white. He had the sharp chest keel as the others, except the others did not have bony plates on their chest. He did. Plus he had an extra finger. Even so, extra finger, black fur, brown scales, chest armor, was this bad?

His head, neck and back also had bony plates and along his spine was a row of sharp spurs. He could not see these characteristics, and even if he did, he still would not understand what was wrong.

It is deformed and sickly, the wrinkled one croaked to his mother. *If it reaches breeding age it will spread its deformity onto its offspring. The Flock will weaken and die. Kill it.*

The fifth hatchling sensed his father's unease with the wrinkled one's decision, yet his father said nothing.

The hatchling's mother agreed. He must be killed. But she couldn't bring herself to do it.

Your first impulse is to protect your offspring, the wrinkled one croaked. *Be strong. Fight your impulse. Save the bloodline. Kill it.*

His mother steeled herself for doing the deed.

19

The two juveniles warbled in chorus, *Human fodder! Human fodder! Kill it! Kill it!* Around and around their song went as they circled over the nest.

The fifth hatchling's mother grabbed him with her beak and whipped him side to side to snap his neck. His vision blurred. His little head tossed side to side, but the armor circling his neck saved the cervical vertebrae from snapping.

His mother dropped him onto the hard ground, outside the nest, and tried stabbing him with her beak. He scrambled to get up on all fours so he could scurry away but no sooner he got half way up she smashed him flat onto his belly. The point of her beak chipped his back plates. Eventually she would pierce his armor.

Hatred for his mother erupted inside him. When she drew back to stab him again he was ready for her. He flipped over and grabbed her beak as she stabbed at him. She tried to fling him off but his opposable thumbs helped him hold on to her. He scaled her beak and raked his claws across her eye. She yelped. Her head twisted sharply. The fifth hatchling lost his grip. His tiny body bounced on the hard soil and rolled to a stop in a cloud of dust.

Regaining his senses, he got up on all fours and hissed at the other giants to stay back.

The giants stared at him, stunned.

The one with the wrinkled neck pulled her head back to try to stab him with her beak. He flapped up into the air, cawing with his infant voice, heading for her milky, yellow eyes.

After seeing what happened to the other giant, the old one stumbled backward in retreat. She covered her face.

The fifth hatchling tore into the leathery old wing, flaking off more skin.

The giant with the yellow fingers clucked to his father, *Do something! It's your offspring!*

The fifth hatchling was too much in a fury to hear his father's response. The juveniles fluttered around him, cheering him on with a new song: *Tear up the old bird! Tear her up!*

The wrinkled one cawed, *Enough! The deformed hatchling shall live.*

It was too late to quell the fifth hatchling's rage. He was not going to stop until the old beast gasped her last breath. His father plucked him off the old one's wing with his beak. His gentle touch calmed the fifth hatchling. It was the first tenderness anyone had shown him since he had hatched.

His father placed him on the ground beside the nest, not in it with the other hatchlings.

The fifth hatchling felt unwelcomed. Out of defiance he crawled back into the nest. One of his siblings shuffled over to him on wobbly limbs to check on him. He sensed that she wanted to see if he was all right.

After the way the adults had treated him, he distrusted her motives.

Sensing his suspicion, she returned to the other hatchlings.

The adults gathered around the nest again. They were resigned to the fact that they were stuck with this malformed newborn, for now, until they figured out what to do with him. His mother had her injured eye pinched shut. Blood collected along the eyelid. With her good eye she glared at him, angry that he, her own offspring, attacked her.

Did she forget that she had tried to kill him? What was he supposed to do? The fifth hatchling refused to look at her. As far as he was concerned he no longer had a mother, and he could sense from her that as far as she was concerned she had only four hatchlings. He had yet to see his first sunset and already he felt alone in this new world.

The fifth hatchling learned the names of his Flock mates. The one who he no longer acknowledged as his mother was called White Sail. His father was Male. The sibling who checked to see if he was all right was Razor Beak. The peeping one was called Peeps. The other two siblings had yet to be named as well as the two juveniles. The yellow fingered one with sores on its face was called Yellow Claws. His Flock mates were not pure white. They had bright pink wing tips and yellow markings in various places, under the arms, around the base of the neck, and so forth. The markings were small, often no larger than a single finger. In Yellow Claws' case, her entire hand was brightly hued. They also had a mane of gray fur running down their backs.

The old one, the one he hated almost as much as his mother, was Flaking Scales, the grand matriarch. The fifth hatchling detested her authority and had contempt for the other adults for giving the beast so much reverence.

Flaking Scales named him Brown Scale.

Yellow Claws contested her decision because the fifth hatchling's color was hardly his most distinctive characteristic. His claws were as sharp as Razor Beak's bite. She thought "Flesh Ripper" would be more suitable, or "Five Fingers". He did have an extra digit. But then his body armor rivaled a crab's. "Crab Shell" would work just as well, she thought.

Flaking Scales rejected her suggestions. The fifth hatchling's name must be dull to dissuade females from mating with him.

His father interjected that if the grand matriarch wanted the fifth hatchling to have a bland name, they could call the brown imp "Male" instead and he could go by "Rainbow Sail".

Flaking Scales snorted, and that was as far as the discussion went.

And so the fifth hatchling became known as Brown Scale.

The afternoon waned and Brown Scale saw his first star. As the sun continued to sink below the horizon another star became visible. Before long the sky was full of stars. They fascinated him. Each one seemed to be a solitary soul, like him. All alone. Yet they did not seem to be afraid of being by themselves. He suspected they liked it. Perhaps being alone was good. Brown Scale needed someone to look up to. He decided he would look up to the stars.

The one who was no longer his mother chittered to the brood that it was time to sleep. She stepped into the nest. Brown Scale's siblings gathered around her to share in her warmth. White Sail paused with one foot still outside the nest when she realized she would be sharing space with "the deformed one". An awkward moment unfolded as it was customary for the newborns to sleep in the nest. Brown Scale did not want to share space with the one who he refused to acknowledge either, yet his instincts told him his survival depended upon remaining within the nest.

White Sail pulled in her last foot into the nest and scrunched herself up so her body would not come in contact with his. Brown Scale curled into a ball on the far side of the nest. The night's cold breath made him shiver. His blood flooded his core to keep his organs warm, leaving his extremities to the mercy of the dropping temperatures. No matter how hard he tucked in his limbs, his wingtips and toes turned miserably cold. He sighed, closed his eyes, and managed as best he could.

After the morning sun warmed him back to where he was comfortable, Brown Scale forgot about how cold the night was. His mother had flown away and left their father to watch the nest. His siblings studied him out of curiosity. He could sense in their minds that they were getting the idea that he might be their leader. The adults had Flaking Scales as their leader. She was the tallest and the oldest. She was the most different from the other adults. He was the most different among the hatchlings.

Peeps peeped, *Hatchling Leader.*

The other siblings joined her, peeping, *Hatchling Leader.*

Brown Scale felt welcomed for once.

Male nudged Brown Scale's siblings with his beak to quiet them. Flaking Scales glared at the nest from her perch on the nearby hill. The hatchlings kept peeping, oblivious to the grand matriarch's disapproval. Their father uttered a sort of clicking sound in his throat which translated to, *he's not your leader.*

Razor Beak bit the tip of his beak in defiance. She knew from the way the females treated her father that she did not have to obey him.

Male turned to Flaking Scales with a disarming look of "I'm trying. I really am!"

White Sail returned, casting her shadow across the nest as she came in for a landing. Brown Scale smelled an appetizing odor from her mouth. He and his siblings realized without needing to be told that she had brought them food. They opened their mouths to her. For each she deposited a portion of chewed fish and seaweed from her throat pouch to their tiny beaks, except for Brown Scale. He received nothing. She didn't even glance in his direction. After Razor Beak, Peeps, and the rest filled their bellies, White Sail swallowed the leftovers.

Brown Scale felt dejected, and hungry.

When night came he had to overcome his cold wingtips and toes, and the gnawing ache in his empty belly. Sleep did not come easily. He spent much of the evening looking up at his friends in the sky, the stars. They did not strike him as beings that needed food. He wished all the more he could be like them—on his own and never hungry.

The following day White Sail fed everyone but him. The same happened the next day, and the next. Flaking Scales clucked in approval. A way had been found in killing Brown Scale. Just let him starve.

Brown Scale became thin and weak as his siblings became strong. He peeped, *I'm hungry*. His siblings backed away from him. They sensed death coming.

Anticipation stirred in the nest when White Sail took off to get the morning meal. Brown Scale's hunger left him depressed. Food was coming and he was not going to get any.

Then Male flew away, leaving the nest unguarded.

Peeps started peeping in alarm.

Razor Beak needled her peeping sister with her beak to shut up. She was confident that they were not in any danger. After all, Flaking Scales and Yellow Claws were in sight. They would not let anyone attack the nest.

Brown Scale became worried that she would turn her powerful beak on him. He tried to stop himself from bleating, *I'm hungry*, but couldn't. His belly hurt too much.

A great shadow fell upon the nest as one of their parents returned. It was their father. This time he had the delicious smell coming from his mouth. He offered Brown Scale food. Brown Scale laid on his belly. He could barely raise his head to receive it. Male deposited a mouthful next to his beak. Brown Scale gobbled up the regurgitated mix of fish and seaweed.

His brother and sisters shuffled toward his meal with greedy eyes.

Male blocked them with his wing then deposited another mouthful of food.

Flaking Scales flew down from her perch atop the hill and landed at the nest, cawing in anger.

Male ignored his matriarch.

Flaking Scales puffed out her chest in a huff. Her moral authority failed to influence him. She took on a threatening stance, yet Male continued to feed his starving son, behaving as though he did not see her.

After Brown Scale had his fill, Male swallowed the rest of the food. Brown Scale's brother and sisters stopped shunning him. They could sense that he was no longer going to die.

Brown Scale's mother was furious with his father for feeding him. His father stood his ground on the basis that he had the right to feed his young. Not even Flaking Scales could stop his father from feeding him. That was how sacred the rules were. They could override the wishes of the individual.

Flaking Scales ordered Male to mate with Yellow Claws. Normally, the father remained paired with the mother until the hatchlings were strong enough to leave the nest. But because White Sail had only one acceptable male for breeding it was important to get another brood hatched as quickly as possible. If all went well, the second hatching would produce another male.

That would improve the odds of there being a male available as the two broods reached breeding age.

Consequently, Brown Scale's father would not be able to feed him because his obligation would switch from White Sail's nest to Yellow Claws'.

There was a sentiment going through the Flock that Flaking Scales wanted to get the second brood hatched right away in order to stop Male from feeding Brown Scale. Brown Scale picked up on that sentiment. He glowered at the grand matriarch as she sat supreme atop her hill.

Male called to one of the juveniles. Brown Scale saw the juvenile fly over to his father. His father and the juvenile then flew over the ridge and down to the beach where they could not be seen. Flaking Scales flew down to the beach to check on them. Brown Scale heard them cawing at each other and then a sharp hiss. The hiss was Flaking Scales'. He couldn't miss her raspy voice.

Then his father flew up over the ridge and hurried over to Yellow Claws, who was prepping her nest.

The juvenile bolted over the ridge and flew to her sister. Her sister clucked at her, eager to hear what happened. The first juvenile kept quiet.

Flaking Scales returned to her perch, satisfied that she had restored order to the Flock.

Brown Scale itched with curiosity. Nothing further developed and the daily routine returned. The sun set. His friends reappeared in the night sky. Brown Scale weathered the falling temperature much better now that he had been fed, but he knew this comfort would not last long. Soon he would be hungry again now that his father was assigned to Yellow Claws' nest.

White Sail took off to get breakfast for everyone but Brown Scale. Brown Scale braced himself for the coming hunger.

The first juvenile sister pressed her head against her sister's. Brown Scale sensed that there was some sort of communication happening. This could be a way to talk to someone in secret. He decided to give it a try and picked Razor Beak. Pressing his head against hers he asked with just his thoughts, no clucks or hissing, *how are you?*

Razor Beak pulled her head back in surprise. She narrowed her gaze at him in suspicion. Once she realized he did not harm her, she tentatively pressed her head against his and repeated the question with just her thoughts, *how are you?*

Hungry, he replied.

Razor Beak pulled away, blinked in thought, and then pressed her head against her unnamed sister's to speak to her with her mind. The unnamed hatchling's eyes opened wide in surprise. She pulled away at first and then put her head against Razor Beak's to hear more. Before long all four of the white hatchlings were trying out this new ability.

Flaking Scales raised her sail in anger and cawed at them to settle down.

Once White Sail's hatchlings stopped talking to each other in secret, Flaking Scales lowered her sail. She didn't take her eye off them, though.

Then the first juvenile landed at the nest with the smell of food coiling around her beak. She locked her gaze with Brown Scale to get his attention. There was a mischievous glint in her eye. Brown Scale figured out what had happened down at the beach. His father had convinced the juvenile to feed him.

She belched out an octopus. It landed before Brown Scale with its tentacles twisting in endless streams of jelly. Brown Scale pecked at it and found it to be too big and rubbery to eat.

The juvenile cawed, taking delight in disappointing him.

It was food nonetheless and Brown Scale was determined to survive. He grabbed it, something that would not be possible if he did not have an opposable thumb, and called to Razor Beak to chop it up into bite-sized morsels with her beak. She did so.

The juvenile blinked, taken aback at how the brown hatchling had foiled her prank. She took advantage of his ingenuity and grabbed a morsel for herself. The other hatchlings joined the feast.

Flaking Scales flew down from her hill, screeching. The juvenile barely took off in time before the grand matriarch could land on top of her. To be sure Brown Scale did not get anything more to eat, Flaking Scales gobbled up the rest of the octopus and then flew back toward her perch.

No sooner had she turned her back, the other juvenile darted across the landscape from the opposite direction and landed at the nest to drop a second octopus. Brown Scale grabbed it and Razor Beak started chopping it into bite-size portions. Flaking Scales noticed the second juvenile taking off from the nest when she landed back on her perch atop the hill. Hissing in frustration, she descended upon the nest, spotted the second octopus, and grabbed it out of Brown Scale's grasp.

The hatchlings peeped in alarm.

Yellow Claws and Male flew to the nest.

The two juveniles buzzed Flaking Scales, cawing, *Food stealer! Food stealer!*

Flaking Scales scrambled into the air and back up to her perch. In her haste to deny Brown Scales anything to eat, she had committed a grave offense: she had taken food from a hatchling.

An unbearable cacophony of accusations and counter accusations screeched between Flaking Scales and the juveniles. Yellow Claws and Male were still under the impression the nest had been attacked by an intruder and searched the area for tracks.

White Sail returned in the midst of the turmoil with a full throat sack. She checked on her hatchlings and saw that they were unharmed and then turned to Flaking Scales for an explanation.

Flaking Scales accused the juveniles of dumping vermin into the nest.

White Sail turned to the juveniles for their side of the story.

The juveniles offered none. They flew out to sea, cackling.

White Sail narrowed her eyes in suspicion at them and then fed her hatchlings with the exception of Brown Scale. They were not particularly hungry, which proved that something had happened while she was away. Yellow Claws and Male could give no explanation either. They had just heard the alarm.

Brown Scale managed to eat enough octopus to take the edge off his hunger pains. By nightfall he ached for more food. He nibbled at the palm tree fronds lining the bottom of the nest. His mother smacked his beak with hers to get him to stop. He waited for her to fall asleep and resumed nibbling the unsatisfying vegetable matter.

3

The two juveniles kept sneaking food to Brown Scale. They came at night, at odd hours, while the others slept. Flaking Scales tried to catch them in the act. But she was old and they were young. The juveniles could stay up all night while Flaking Scales succumbed to fatigue. She warned White Sail to watch out for the juveniles. White Sail kept vigil for a few nights and then decided it was not worth the effort. She had disowned the brown imp and she was not going to waste any more time and effort on him.

The food the juveniles brought was not always suitable. They dropped off giant clams, which he had to pry open to get at the delicacy inside and if his grip slipped the shells snapped shut, and if his head was in too deep when they closed... Other nights they would bring too little, like one strand of seaweed. The juveniles could care less about his welfare. They did what they did to be aggravating.

Nevertheless he survived. His arms grew twice the length of his legs and the fourth finger on his hands, the "membrane finger" as the humans called it, grew even longer. By the time he saw his second full moon, he and his siblings were big enough to keep each other warm. Their mother slept outside the nest.

During the day, they took turns flapping their wings to loosen the cramps in their muscles. The nest could no longer contain them. It was time to explore a new frontier. Brown Scale took the first step outside of the nest, planting one tentative hand on the hard, black regolith. It felt strange. He had not been outside the nest since birth. To him that was a lifetime ago.

His siblings cheered him on, chirping, *Hatchling Leader. Hatchling Leader. Hatchling Leader.*

Encouraged by their chant, Brown Scale climbed out of the nest.

His brother and sisters cawed in praise of his courage.

He called to them to come out.

Peeps, surprisingly, accepted the challenge. After she climbed out she stood stock still, shivering from fright.

White Sail rubbed her neck to show how proud she was.

The last three hatchlings scrambled out of the nest.

White Sail clucked, *you are hatchlings no more. Today you are juveniles.*

Her brood held their heads up with pride.

Brown Scale noticed that his father was craning his neck to watch what was happening. He could not join White Sail to share in this important moment because he had to remain at Yellow Claws' nest. Yellow Claws was roosting on her eggs.

Brown Scale remembered what his father had done to keep him fed. *I survived,* he called out to Male in loud clucks. *I am a juvenile now!*

Male acknowledged him with a swan-like bob of his head.

White Sail flapped her wings. Holding herself aloft in the air, she seemed to hover over their heads and landed on the opposite side of the nest. Naturally, her brood wanted to imitate her and flapped their wings. Razor Beak made it into the air and started flying from the nest. She squawked in surprise, drew her arms in tight along her sides, and crashed into the dirt. Getting back up, she walked back to the nest with pebbles stuck in her fur.

Their mother repeated the same trick, flapping over their heads and landed on the opposite side of the nest. Peeps, the unnamed male and female flapped again. The male managed to get a meter off the ground. Out of habit, Brown Scale scrutinized the situation first. His mother had made flying seem effortless. The trick was to capture as much air with the wing membranes.

Swinging the arms was not good enough. Brown Scale outstretched his arms, spreading his membranes, and then flapped with force and purpose. His wings captured the air and he rose off the ground. He lacked his mother's finesse, yet he managed to get airborne with half as many flaps.

White Sail chirped to show how pleased she was in their effort. She turned and walked away from the nest. Without having to be told, Brown Scale and the others followed her toward the ridge to be taught on how to fly. Before they got far White Sail glanced over her shoulder. When she saw Brown Scale, she spun around and planted her wing in front of him, blocking him from going any further. With her bad eye, the one he had injured, she glared at him. It was all she needed to do to communicate to him that she was not going to train him.

Brown Scale fell out of line.

The rest followed their mother to the ridge. White Sail summoned the two juveniles, who were now called the Gray Sisters. The two juvenile females had grown at an exponential rate since Brown Scale had hatched, sprouting from three meters to forty meters in height. Their wings spanned over a hundred meters. They were nearly old enough to be counted as matriarchs. Their fur and scales had turned to the same color of gray as the mane that ran down their backs. Hence they were called the Gray Sisters. Their wing membranes darkened as well, but not as much and their sails were now a bright yellow. Their color change had caused anxiety among the adults. Flaking Scales assured them that she had seen this happen before, long before the other adults had been born. It was rare, but acceptable.

White Sail instructed her brood to pay attention while the Gray Sisters demonstrated how to take flight.

The Gray Sisters sized up the task at hand, wiggled their butts, sized up the task some more, and then flapped their wings wildly. Pretending to lose their balance, they plunged down the sloop.

White Sail clenched her beak and growled.

Brown Scale could hear the echo of the Sisters cackling from the bottom of the slope on the other side of the ridge.

White Sail's brood cackled too.

The Gray Sisters flew back up to the ridge and clucked, *that is how it is done. You try.*

White Sail rebuked them with a sharp hiss.

Her children recoiled in fear.

The Gray Sisters put on an air of innocence.

White Sail bobbed her head three times to draw the youngsters' attention. She extended the sail atop her head and leapt into the air with one flap. After two more flaps she went into a glide. Her form diminished in the distance. Turning her head slightly, she swung around and glided back to the ridge, landing with grace.

Brown Scale was dismayed. Flying defined what it meant to be a pterosaur. It was depressing to think he would be stuck shuffling around on all fours.

His father called him over to Yellow Claws' nest.

Brown Scale started shuffling over.

Male raised the sail atop his head and flapped his wings, signaling to Brown Scale that he should fly, not walk.

Brown Scale couldn't believe his father expected him to fly over to him. He had not been taught.

Then he sensed his father's thoughts in his mind. *Your body knows what to do. You were born to fly. Fortify your courage. That is all your mother is teaching your brother and sisters, to fortify their courage. Look.*

Brown Scale looked, and watched. The youngsters gripped the ridge, reluctant to take flight, while White Sail outstretched her wings to entice them to imitate her again. When that didn't work, she gently nudged them with her beak. His father was right. All White Sail was doing was encouraging them.

Male held his wings up, prompting Brown Scale to give it a go.

What about landing, Brown Scale asked in thought.

Just land. Trust yourself.

Brown Scale repeated what he did before. He lifted off the ground. His feet hung loose underneath him. The empty nest shrank as he rose higher and higher. Soon he rose above Flaking Scales' hilltop perch and then Flaking Scales herself. Male thrust his wings out to his side. Brown Scale did the same and broke into a smooth, effortless glide. He dove toward his father and swooshed past him.

Open your sail, Male clucked at him as he passed.

The sail! Brown Scale had forgotten. He raised the sail atop his head. Within minutes he figured out how to use it to adjust his course. He performed a circle around his father and then flew toward the ridge and soared over his siblings. Once he passed the ridge he was shocked at how high he was in the air. He did not even cast a shadow on the ground. Within a heartbeat he was over the marching waves of the sea. The experience was exhilarating and transcendent. He could no longer see himself as a ground dweller. The sky was his home. Yet, his instincts told him he should not fly too far into unexplored territory alone. He considered going back to the island when he heard Razor Beak caw. He lowered his sail and looked over his shoulder, seeing all four of his siblings following behind him. Turning his head forward, he led them a little further out before returning to the ridge where White Sail was waiting. She was miffed that her brood followed the brown imp's lead rather than hers. Brown Scale's siblings were too giddy after their first successful flight to sense her disappointment.

Brown Scale left them to be with his father.

Male tapped him on the head with the tip of his beak to congratulate him on a job well done. He coached Brown Scale further in the succeeding days. There were several types of flapping. The first kind got you up into the air. The second increased speed. The third increased altitude while in flight. Once those three types were mastered, they could be mixed, matched, and modified to perform any number of aerial maneuvers.

Brown Scale mastered the three types of flying. The thought occurred to him that he could go off on his own now that he could fly and feed himself. Yet, his instincts cautioned that he should remain with the Flock until he reached adult size. In the meantime there would be new lessons to learn.

Yellow Claws hatched her four eggs and when her offspring were ready she trained them on how to fly. The added numbers strengthened the Flock's mental link to the point where communicating via telepathy became more convenient than clucking and cawing, and their ability to think and devise plans increased in sophistication. The only problem the Flock had, from Flaking Scales' perspective, was the brown imp. She did not want his seed contaminating the bloodline. He needed to be killed before he reached breeding age.

Flaking Scales dispatched the Gray Sisters to scout the surrounding sea for predators and human activity. Three days later the sisters returned. They landed atop the hill and showed their memories to the grand matriarch.

Flaking Scales saw mental images of human machines sailing their usual routes. None of the sisters' memories revealed any predators. The Flock appeared to be safe, although the sisters spotted one thing of interest.

They had flown out to their old island and spotted a human fighting machine anchored off the coast. The Two-Headed One was as much an enemy of the humans as it was of the Flock. Flaking Scales deduced that the humans must be tracking the Two-Headed One.

White Sail's and Yellow Claws' offspring could reach the ship. That gave Flaking Scales an idea on how to get rid of Brown Scale.

She called White Sail and Yellow Claws to the hilltop. The matriarchs put their heads together so they could communicate in private. The Gray Sisters recalled their memories of their scouting mission for White Sail and Yellow Claws. Flaking Scales ordered the matriarchs to focus on the fighting machine off the coast of their old nesting ground.

It is time for the juveniles to go on their first raid, Flaking Scales stated in thought. *Attack that machine.*

Yellow Claws pulled her head away and clucked in alarm.

Flaking Scales drew in her breath in a sharp hiss to admonish her for breaking the circle.

Yellow Claws pressed her head back in contact with the others.

We didn't attack a fighting machine on our first raid, she said in thought. *Why should our offspring? They will be slaughtered.*

White Sail agreed.

This may be our last chance to kill the deformed one, Flaking Scales insisted.

I will not sacrifice my brood just to kill the one I have disowned, White Sail said.

Neither will I, Yellow Claws added.

Look how your offspring follow behind Brown Scale, Flaking Scales told them. *Look!*

White Sail and Yellow Claws broke the circle to watch their offspring fly over the sea. Wherever Brown Scale flew, the rest followed. They turned back to reform the circle.

When Brown Scale attacks, Flaking Scales said, *the offspring will fall in behind him. The humans will kill him first because he is in the lead. Once they do, call your offspring out of the range of the human weapons and bring them home. Then the Gray Sisters and I will find easier prey for your offspring.*

The more White Sail and Yellow Claws considered Flaking Scales' plan the more they liked it, especially White Sail. Finally, she will be able to rid herself of the shame of being the mother of a deformed offspring.

4

Every morning Brown Scale leapt into the sky and soared as far as he could out over the barren sea. He never got far before his siblings were following his tail. They persisted in seeing him as their leader. He liked them, but he liked being alone more. After Yellow Claws' offspring learned to fly, they started following him, too. They were drawn by his distinctive appearance. Once he had his uninvited entourage, flying out to sea lost its thrill.

He tried to escape from them, but they kept pace. Eventually their following him turned into a series of games. There was Match the Maneuver where he tried to shake them by performing sharp turns and sudden dives and swerves. Then there was the simple Chase where they tried to keep up with him. Once in a while he managed to get far enough ahead to hide in the outcroppings along the island's coast. He waited until someone spotted him and called out his position. Then he darted back into the air and the game resumed.

After another carefree day, Brown Scale landed on the beach with his siblings. Razor Beak cawed, *You will never be able to fly away from us. We will always be with you.*

Brown Scale noticed that their brother and two sisters wandered off to congregate with Yellow Claws' juveniles.

Are you sure, he clucked and flicked his beak toward the others.

Razor Beak turned to look and then turned back to Brown Scale. *Then I will always be with you,* she cawed softly.

Flaking Scales summoned the youngsters of both broods to a meeting atop the hill. Brown Scale followed the other juveniles to see what the meeting was about. Their mothers were also present.

You have learned to fly, Flaking Scales told them in thought. *Now it is time to learn how to fight. The humans are our enemies. They kill us so we must kill them. Their numbers are uncountable. But do not be afraid. Humans are easy to kill. And they are nourishing. Concentrate. I shall show you where our enemy is located.*

The grand matriarch closed her eyes in concentration. Brown Scale and the other juveniles did the same. An image of a machine appeared in their minds. It was gray in color and had a long, narrow shape like a fallen tree. It was resting off the coast of an island. Flaking Scales implanted the knowledge of the island's location into their minds. They could find it as easily as they could find their home island.

Your mothers and the Gray Sisters will accompany you, Flaking Scales telepathically stated. *Follow their instructions. Kill as many humans as you can. There will be many of them and they can attack from a distance. Their weapons are loud. They puff smoke and spit pebbles that can pierce your skin. Observe.*

She shared memories of humans firing their weapons and memories of their machines in battle.

Shall we eat a human as soon as we kill it, Peeps asked using telepathy.

No, Flaking Scales replied. *Eat humans only after you have killed them all. I would be pleased if you brought some back with you. It has been a long while since I tasted human flesh.* In conclusion she reminded them to stick together. *Your ability to think weakens when you are alone. The closer you are together, the wiser you will be.*

The juveniles had no further questions. Flaking Scales dismissed them. White Sail and Yellow Claws went off by themselves to plan the attack. Brown Scale flew down to his father.

Why weren't you at the meeting, he asked telepathically.

I am a male, Male replied. *Males have no say in the affairs of the Flock.*

Did you have to learn how to fight?

Yes. His father shared memories of the raids he had made on the humans when he was a juvenile.

If you learned how to fight, why can't you have a say?

Because an adult male is for breeding only. His purpose is to remain at the nesting grounds where he will be safe. It would be different if there were more of us males. The Flock can afford to lose a breeding age female, but it cannot afford to lose a breeding age male. So the females have a responsibility to ensure our survival. Those of us who are being protected must submit to our protectors. That is how the world works.

Then why are we expected to learn how to fight when we are young?

Everyone must learn how to fight. You are useless if you are unable to fight.

That does not make sense. If you share the same risks as a female you should have the same say as a female.

His father leaned close to him and peered deep into his mind. *Our customs do not make sense to you because you hate the matriarchs.*

Brown Scale was unsure if he should interpret his father's last comment as a warning or a criticism. He turned and found Razor Beak behind him.

Did you overhear our father?

Razor Beak tipped her beak to indicate that she had.

Brown Scale waited to see if his hatred for the matriarchs would upset her. Everyone revered the matriarchs.

She didn't mind. The hostility between him and the matriarchs had been a staple in her life since birth. That was just the way things were.

They joined Peeps and their unnamed brother and sister.

You have already been in a fight, Peeps said to Brown Scale and Razor Beak. *We will follow you.*

Follow Hatchling Leader, Razor Beak replied. *I only fought in one battle. Brown Scale has been fighting to survive his entire life.*

They started clucking, *Hatchling Leader. Hatchling Leader.*

Yellow Claws' juveniles shuffled over to see what the clucking was about.

Peeps explained. *Brown Scale fought two matriarchs and survived. His mother tried to starve him and he survived. He was the first to leave the nest. He was the first to fly. He is our hatchling leader.*

Yellow Claws' brood joined the chant.

The two mothers summoned their broods into the air and together with the Gray Sisters they flew to their old island where the Flock colony once lived. The juveniles were in awe. Their island home had a single hill while this one had an entire mountain range. The range formed the southeast portion of the island. White Sail and Yellow Claws flew toward the mountains to cover their approach. They landed amongst the cliffs.

The humans use invisible waves like bats to see long distances, White Sail explained telepathically. *The waves cause your skin to tingle when they touch you. When you feel that tingling, the humans have found you. Did any of you feel any tingling?*

The juveniles chittered no, they did not feel a thing.

Good. Their machine should be on the other side of the island. Peeps, fly up to the rise. See if the machine is still there.

Peeps fluttered up to the ridge and peeked over the top. Gliding back down, she peeped excitedly, *I saw it! I saw the machine! It is in the water near the shore.*

Find a place to roost. We attack at dawn. The humans will be groggy then.

The juveniles exhaled in relief. Their arms were sore. It took all day to cross the ocean to reach this island.

Brown Scale saw his mother fly to a cliff and hunch over something that was on the ground. Yellow Claws rested her beak on White Sail's shoulder in sympathy. After a while Yellow Claws flew away to find a place to roost, leaving White Sail alone. Curious, he clung to the near-vertical slope and clawed his way over to another cliff where he could see what his mother was looking at. Razor Beak followed him. They saw a pile of blackened bones. Their mother's eyes were closed. A sorrowful chitter sounded in her throat.

One of the Gray Sisters landed behind Brown Scale and Razor Beak.

The bones are her brother's, the Gray Sister said in thought.

She led Brown Scale and Razor Beak to a gap in the peeks where they could see the western slope of the mountain. Here the mountainside had a gentle gradient. A jungle covered the foothills below. The verdant flora gave the air a healthy scent. *My nest was over there. The view overlooked the trees. It was a beautiful place.*

Brown Scale could sense that she missed her old home, although he could not tell which nest was hers as there were scores of nests along the slope. All of them contained scorched eggs or blackened bones. He asked what happened to the colony.

The Gray Sister flew down to a valley between the mountains. Brown Scale and Razor Beak followed her. They found her standing beside an enormous footprint of a three-toed beast. The toes were short and thick.

This is what happened, the Gray Sister stated in thought.

Show us your memories of the creature that made this footprint, Razor Beak said.

The Gray Sister shuddered. *No. The footprint is enough,* she said. *I will tell you his name. Everyone in the animal kingdom knows it. You should too. He is called the Two-Headed One.* She abruptly took off to join her sister.

Brown Scale and Razor Beak looked at each other and wondered how horrible could this creature have been.

In the morning, White Sail and Yellow Claws showed memories of how they had killed humans to give their broods tips on how to fight. The juveniles were eager to go on the attack, except for Brown Scale. He was not interested in scoring a victory for the matriarchs. To him the raid was a lesson in survival. Nothing more.

Slaughter the humans, White Sail cawed.

Slaughter them, Yellow Claws chimed telepathically. *The humans look like apes but they breed like rats. They have taken the best nesting grounds. Because of them we must lay our eggs on small islands, leaving little room for us to build a colony.*

The juveniles whipped themselves into a frenzy, cawing, *Slaughter them! Slaughter them!*

Brown Scale leapt from his perch and dived for the sea. Razor Beak and Peeps fell in behind him, flying side by side, followed by the rest of the juveniles. Just before striking the water, Brown Scale leveled off and skimmed the waves. He swooped around the mountains into full view of the human machine. Its weapons hummed as they turned toward the incoming pterosaurs and opened fire. The rounds shot overhead. Not one juvenile was hit. Brown Scale had planned it that way. He had noticed from the Gray Sisters' memories that the humans had built their smoke puffers to shoot at tall prey or prey coming in from the sky, not for prey that was small and coming in low.

Peeps, Razor Beak, he ordered telepathically, *attack the smoke puffers from the left.*

They acknowledged him with a caw.

Brown Scale swung around to the machine's right flank and then swung up onto its back. There were two smoke puffers. The larger of the two fired with a rhythmic sounding *thump! Thump! Thump!* It was too slow and unwieldy to be a threat. The smaller one was agile and spewed a steady stream of pebbles. He grabbed the smaller smoke puffer's tubes and tried to force it to shoot its pebbles into the bigger smoke puffer, but the tubes were scalding hot. Hissing in surprise, he released the tubes.

At the same time, Peeps and Razor Beak flew into view from the machine's left flank. They pecked the upper body of the smaller smoke puffer, piercing its smooth skin. By then the other juveniles were swarming over the machine. The small smoke puffer twisted and spewed a stream of pebbles into Pearly White, who was one of Yellow Claws' offspring. Within an instant the pebbles punched dozens of holes into her body. Blood splattered across her white fur. She let out a screech as the stream blew her out over the waves. She dropped into the sea, flailing to stay afloat.

Brown Scale and his sisters clung to the twisting machine as they pecked feverishly. They tore away the skin covering the upper body and plunged their beaks into the smoke puffer's guts. Electric sparks popped out of the thing's gizzard followed by acrid smoke. The puffer's hum fell silent. Its tubes spewed no more pebbles.

We killed it, Peeps cawed, thrilled by their first victory.

The other juveniles cawed out in alarm. *Humans! Humans! Humans!*

Eight humans gathered on an upper level of the machine. They fired pebbles at them with sticks. Razor Beak took a hit to the right shoulder and arm. Both hits drew blood. One pebble grazed Peeps' cheek, leaving a streak of bare flesh. But Brown Scale was unharmed. Despite their sting, the pebbles bounced off his armored skin.

He cawed to his sisters, *stay behind me.*

His sisters followed behind him as he flew to the upper deck. A human aimed his pebble-shooter at him. Their eyes locked. Brown Scale could see the ape-like creature was fierce and cunning. Its faith in its stick was unflinching. Fire flashed from the stick's tip as the pebbles popped out and pecked at his armor. Before the human realized its weapon was ineffective, Brown Scale grabbed him by the neck with his beak and gave the creature a sharp twist. The cervical vertebrae snapped and the human went limp in his grasp.

Razor Beak and Peeps sprung out from behind him and scored their first human kills. All across the deck a melee broke out between the humans and juveniles. In the end, the juveniles were swifter. The humans lay dead.

Despite their wounds, the juveniles' spirits were unbroken. They gorged themselves on the corpses, tearing away the tasteless outer skin to get at the sweet meat underneath.

Brown Scale ignored his gnawing appetite and searched his surroundings. Surely, there had to be more humans than this.

He spotted them—on the island, near the jungle. They had set up a half dozen habitats. A flying machine was parked outside their encampment.

He cawed out the battle cry: *Humans! Humans! Humans!*

The juveniles raised their heads from their feast, and looked in the direction he was looking. They cawed in excitement.

Brown Scale paused to regard one of the pebble shooters and then looked at his hand, and then the human hands. They had opposable thumbs like him. Maybe he could use a human tool as well as they could. He picked up a pebble shooter with his beak and flew after the juveniles. Pumping his wings, he passed them and landed outside the encampment. He had spanned the distance too quickly for the humans to score any hits but once he was on the ground they concentrated their fire on him. Their pebbles ricocheted off his armored plates. He dropped the pebble shooter on the ground and grasped it in his hand. Once he pointed it at the humans they gasped in shock. However, his shooter failed to shoot any pebbles. Neither did it matter because the humans fled toward the jungle. The juveniles pounced on them before they could reach the trees. Shortly, they turned their enemies into a second feast.

Brown Scale dropped his shooter and stared at it, wondering why it did not shoot pebbles.

Razor Beak helped him in his examination. Neither of them could puzzle out how it worked.

Then they heard the waterborne machine turn its big smoke puffer. Brown Scale saw that the puffer was aiming toward the encampment. Both he and his sister called out the alarm to flee.

The juveniles took to the air just as the big smoke puffer opened fire. Its rounds exploded in the encampment, blowing the dead humans apart. That worked out in the juveniles' favor because the smaller pieces were easier to carry. In between volleys they doubled back to grab a prize and flew to the mountains.

Brown Scale picked up the pebble shooter with his beak while Razor Beak grabbed a portion of meat. Together they returned to their mother.

The juveniles offered the meat to their mothers as gifts. White Sail and Yellow Claws gratefully accepted their offerings. White Sail hissed when she saw Brown Scale return to his perch. She demanded to see the offsprings' memories of the battle. Brown Scale was close enough to peer into the mental exchange. Yellow Claws chittered in distress when she saw that Pearly White had been shot out of the sky. White Sail snorted at her to settle down. They should be grateful that only one offspring had been killed. After seeing how successful the raid had been, she scowled back up at Brown Scale, angry that he had survived. It became clear in the mental contact that the point of the raid was to get him killed. Instead Pearly White paid the price.

Brown Scale scowled back at her. Out of defiance he flew back around to the northeast side of the island with the pebble shooter in his mouth and searched the shoreline. There on the beach he found Yellow Claws' lost daughter. She was crying for help.

The humans were back out in the open, picking up their half-eaten dead from the deck of their machine. They yelled when they spotted Brown Scale and fired their pebble-shooting sticks. He pointed his shooter at the humans. They fled from sight. Putting the human-made tool back into his mouth, he grabbed the dying offspring with his feet and flew back to Yellow Claws' roost. He laid Pearly White before Yellow Claws.

Pearly White had hung limp in his grip, but the sight of her mother renewed her strength. She pulled up on shaky limbs, took three steps toward Yellow Claws, and slumped onto her belly.

Yellow Claws stroked her with the tip of her beak and cooed soothingly to her. The little one's siblings gathered around. She was going to die, but she was not going to die alone.

Brown Scale flapped over to White Sail's cliff and dropped the pebble shooter before her as his gift.

Peeps, Razor Beak, and the unnamed siblings gazed at Brown Scale's offering with a mix of awe and envy.

Fuming, White Sail knocked the shooter off the cliff. It clattered against the rocks at the bottom of the mountain.

Brown Scale's siblings cawed in protest. White Sail silenced them with a sharp hiss and spoke to them with telepathy.

Yellow Claws and her brood will not leave until Pearly White dies. We cannot abandon them so we must stay too. That will give the machine time to search for us. It is not safe up here on the cliffs. All of you will be at risk of being killed because of the brown imp!

One of the Gray Sisters cawed for attention. She landed on the cliff and showed her memory of what she had just seen on the northeast side of the island. The machine was heading out to sea.

The humans are fleeing, Peeps peeped.

We won, Brown Scale's unnamed brother chirped.

They fled because they are afraid of Brown Scale's pebble shooter, Razor Beak clucked. She started chanting, *Hatchling Leader!*

Peeps and the unnamed siblings joined the chant.

White Sail clenched her fingers, scaring the cliff's rocky surface with long white claw marks.

5

Shindo Yamaguchi arrived at Momokita University. He came to the university to see a friend, but he was also here on business. Under his arm he carried a sealed envelope. The contents were not to be viewed by anyone except for the intended recipient. His friend was the recipient.

A pair of female students in their early twenties gave him sidelong glances as they passed him on the tree-lined path leading to the Science Hall auditorium. Their expressions turned rosy. They liked what they saw. Shindo was a fit man and his black suit and tie added gravitas to his appearance.

He removed his sunglasses when he stepped into the Science Hall and stopped at the admissions table. A middle-aged woman welcomed him with a bow and a smile. "Welcome to our annual Dino Days festival. Here is our schedule of events."

Shindo accepted a brochure from her and then showed her his credentials, giving his last name first, according to Japanese custom.

"Yamaguchi, Shindo, from the Ministry of Defense. I am here to see Professor Yuzo Abe."

"He is giving his lecture now." She motioned toward the closed double doors where a ticket collector stood on duty. "You may go in."

"Thank you." Shindo put his credentials away and was about to head for the double doors when she added:

"The admission fee for his lecture is 1200 yen."

This was a national security matter and she wanted to charge admission? Like a good sport Shindo smiled and pulled out his wallet.

"However, if you would like a one-day pass that will be 8,000 yen. Fifteen thousand for the full weekend."

"Abe's lecture will be fine." He handed her the money.

She handed him his ticket.

"I will take a receipt."

The woman gave him a dumbfounded look. "A receipt?"

"Yes, please."

"We normally don't hand out receipts." The woman smiled.

"I normally don't have to quote the laws regulating commercial transactions. Would you like me to?" If she wanted to be a stickler for the rules, so could he.

The woman sighed. Her fingers banged the keyboard of her laptop as she typed up a receipt, unhappy with the extra work he was putting her through. Shindo had no pity. After all, she started this.

"There." She handed him his receipt as soon as it rolled off her printer.

Shindo smiled again.

She looked away with a frown.

Shindo tucked the receipt into the inside pocket of his jacket and headed for the double doors.

The ticket collector accepted his ticket and opened one of the doors.

Shindo nodded in gratitude and stepped into the dimly lit auditorium. The room could seat a thousand people and out of all of those seats he could count the empty ones with one hand. Abe was always a good draw. Shindo grabbed a chair in back so as not to cause a distraction. It was an uncanny coincidence. Professor Abe was giving a lecture on Flock pterosaurs, and what did Shindo come here to talk to the professor about? Flock pterosaurs.

The image on the projection screen featured illustrations of the heads of a Flock pterosaur and the *Tapejara*, which was a pterodactyl that lived back in the mid Cretaceous.

"It's always been my opinion that the Flock pterosaur is a modern day *Tapejara*. They both have that toucan-like beak. They both have these enormous head crests. The only difference is that the *Tapejara's* crest is a fixed feature while the Flock crest is articulated." Professor Abe indicated each characteristic with his pointer. "It can be folded like a sail when not in use."

He put up illustrations of the two pterosaurs. Both were featured in the same flight pose. "The same can be said for the overall body. Both identical. The only other difference, aside from size, is this." He pointed at the Flock pterosaur's chest. "A Flock pterosaur has an enormous keel, the largest in any known flying animal." He replaced the illustration with a Japanese Defense Force photo of a live Flock adult. "The larger the keel, the more muscle you can attach to it and the Flock pterodactyl has a generous amount of muscle. Its chest looks more like a bodybuilder's chest than a flying reptile's."

The audience laughed, although the professor was exaggerating for effect.

"The extra muscle allows the animal to reach speeds up to one thousand kilometers an hour. The Flock are the fastest airborne creatures on Earth.

"But getting back to the keel, it's so big that it sticks out of the chest and it is sheathed in keratin. The keratin gives it a razor-sharp edge. One of the Flock's favorite tactics is to buzz the heads of their opponents, striking them with the keel. The Flock has been known to crack open the skulls of other kaiju."

Professor Abe went on to describe growth rates, diet, and observed behavior. At the conclusion the lights came back on and the professor answered questions for ten minutes and wrapped up with his thanks for their attendance. The audience applauded. He bowed, set the pointer behind the lectern for the next speaker, and exited through the side door at the front of the room with his presentation materials.

Shindo stepped out through the side door at the back of the room. Abe was waiting for him by the other door.

"I saw you come in," the professor said. "If you were one of my students I would have flunked you for being late."

Shindo smiled sheepishly and bowed out of respect to the eminent paleontologist. "May I have a minute of your time, Professor?"

Professor Abe smiled. "What if I don't have a minute to give you?"

"Then I am afraid that I will have to insist," Shindo stated firmly.

Abe chuckled. "The world is in peril again, is it?"

"I guarantee you are going to find this interesting." Shindo held up the sealed envelope.

"Oh?" the professor replied with a cagey tone.

They went to his office. Abe had fossils that he had excavated back in his youth on display on his book shelf. His most prized fossil was an *Oviraptor* egg, which he kept safe and dust-free under a glass case. This specimen was a gift to him from the American Museum of Natural History. It was one of the eggs discovered by Roy Chapman Andrews himself. A gold-plated plaque confirmed its authenticity.

Abe cleared his desk. Shindo pulled up a chair and sat down opposite from the professor.

"This is the story thus far," Shindo began. "Five weeks ago Tiamatodon had been spotted lurking in the waters near the Ogasawara islands. The *Sakai-maru* had been deployed from her base in Chichijima to track its movements."

"The *Sakai-maru*?" The professor raised his brow.

"The *Sakai-maru* is a Maritime Defense Force destroyer," Shindo explained. "The ship followed Tiamatodon on a south-easterly course. After sailing five hundred kilometers, the captain found an uncharted island where Tiamatodon had stomped through the jungle. Here are aerial photographs taken by the destroyer's helicopter." He removed photographs from the sealed envelope and set them on the desk. "On the shore you can see Tiamatodon's tracks heading into the jungle." He pointed to the tracks in the photo. "Judging by the new growth in Tiamatodon's trail, the recon team estimated that he had made landfall on the island about four months ago."

Abe picked up the photo and raised his glasses to get a better look.

"The tracks led to the mountains where there were scores of Flock nests."

Abe set the first photo down and studied the ones showing the mountain slopes where the Flock colony had placed their nests. Not a one had been spared. All had been scorched by Tiamatodon's plasma rays.

Abe lowered his glasses. "Such a shame. This is the largest colony I have ever seen."

"On the other hand, Tiamatodon has done us a favor. That colony was in striking distance of the Ogasawara Islands."

Abe conceded Shindo's point with a nod. "What happened next?"

"As far as the captain of the *Sakai-maru* was concerned, the island should have been clear of Flock pterosaurs. He sent a team of six to the island to investigate the damage Tiamatodon had done. At 4am, Tokyo time, a group of about ten juvenile pterosaurs attacked the ship. They came around the mountains and flew below the level of the ship's deck. The crews couldn't get a good shot at them. The juveniles destroyed the ship's forward CIWS turret and killed fourteen members of the crew, including the team that had been sent to the island. Now, this is the reason why I am bringing this incident to your attention."

Shindo removed the last six photographs from the envelope. Without saying a word, he placed the best shot of a brown-colored Flock juvenile on top of the others. Abe grabbed the photograph and propped his glasses back up on his forehead. Shindo smiled in satisfaction when he saw how much the image engrossed Abe's attention.

Slowly, Professor Abe set the photograph down on his desk. He stared off into space and exhaled his breath, heavily. Licking his lips he looked at Shindo. "Coffee?"

"No thank you."

"I need a cup." The professor started his coffeemaker.

"You look like you need a brandy."

"Not at my age and with my gut." Abe slapped his paunch. "I don't want diabetes."

"So what do you think?" Shindo nodded at the photo. "Is that a different species or the same one?"

"It's the same species. No doubt about it. You have no idea how significant this is."

"Believe me, Professor, I do. That pterosaur is bulletproof. The captain's men shot at it from point blank range. Their rounds bounced right off. Small arms fire should have killed it. And it's smart. It shielded two of its siblings so they could get in close to attack the crew. Then it picked up an assault rifle and aimed it back at the captain's men. It didn't understand the gun well enough to pull the trigger, but nevertheless it pointed the barrel in the right direction."

The professor examined the remaining photos. "You can see the creature's opposable thumb in this picture. That's why it was able to hold onto the gun. And it's a male. You can tell by the knob at the end of the sail rod. A female's tapers to a sharp point." He set the photos down with the others. "Now what I find significant is that this creature is proof that the Flock is evolving. We first encountered the Flock back in the 1950s and have been fighting them ever since. Unlike other kaiju we can kill a Flock pterosaur. It isn't easy, but it can be done.

"So what does a species do when its survival is threatened? It either goes extinct or it adapts. The new characteristics on this animal," Abe set his finger on the brown juvenile's photo, "are adaptations. Bony plates on the chest, back, neck, and head. Opposable thumb. Heightened intelligence. All the things the Flock needs to survive in battle against our weapons."

"I am glad we are of the same mind on this." Shindo placed the empty envelope on Abe's desk. "Would you be interested in helping me convince my superiors of the danger this animal poses to our security?"

"Of course. What do you need me to do?"

Flaking Scales was frustrated when she saw Brown Scale return from the raid. White Sail and

Yellow Claws landed on her hilltop and gave their report. They put their heads together and secretly shared their memories with their grand matriarch as well as the memories they had gleaned from their broods. What Flaking Scales saw caused her to reconsider Brown Scale's value to the Flock. His tactics allowed the juveniles to get in close to their enemy. His tough skin protected him from the pebble shooters. And his cleverness caused the humans to run rather than fight.

White Sail felt betrayed because Flaking Scales seemed to be having a change of heart.

We must be practical, Flaking Scales said to her telepathically. *He can be useful in helping our offspring survive.*

You never hatched a deformed offspring, White Sail protested. *It's shameful. And to see that he is indestructible only hurts me more. It is like having a scar that will not heal.*

You don't have to be ashamed anymore, Yellow Claws replied. *He brought Pearly White back to me. Her spirit sleeps in peace because of him. I would be proud to have him as my offspring.*

I would give him to you but it would not erase the fact I conceived him.

Leave Brown Scale be, for now, Flaking Scales said. *If we keep trying to kill him, the others will side with him against us. The matriarchy must not be compromised.*

The matriarchy has been compromised. White Sail revealed her memories of what happened after the battle. Brown Scale discovered that the raid was a ploy to kill him. He used the ploy to make himself appear morally superior by returning Pearly White to her mother. As a result he won the adoration of his peers at the expense of the matriarchy's authority. The schism between the offspring and adults was already forming.

I will fix this, Flaking Scales said.

She cawed to the juveniles gathered at the bottom of the hill to give her their attention. When she had it she called Brown Scale before her.

Brown Scale stared blankly up at her.

Come, she cawed.

Brown Scale braced himself, expecting a fight. When she showed no sign of aggression he flew to the hilltop and landed before Flaking Scales. Her sixty-two meter height made him seem like a mortal standing before his god.

Is this true? Flaking Scales shared Razor Beak's memory of him leading the juveniles in the attack. She broadcasted her thoughts to the whole Flock.

Brown Scale confirmed this was true with a chirp.

Why did you fly toward the machine so close to the waves? Flaking Scales asked. *Everyone knows you should attack from the air.*

The machines can't hit you if you are down low. Brown Scale brought up a memory of the waterborne machine, showing how the deck blocked the guns' line of sight.

Well done, Flaking Scales said. *Can anyone name another creature in the animal kingdom who has outwitted the humans?*

No one else in the Flock could think of anyone who had.

You are the first, Flaking Scales said to Brown Scale. *Now tell me, is this also true?* Flaking Scales shared Yellow Claws' memory of him bringing Pearly White to her.

With a chirp, Brown Scale confirmed he did return Yellow Claws' daughter to her.

You honored your mother with your cunning and kindness.

Brown Scale looked to White Sail to see if she really did feel honored.

White Sail narrowed her eyes at Flaking Scales. Her stare was as sharp as a shark's teeth.

You are the pride of our Flock, the grand matriarch continued. *I am pleased with you, Hatchling Leader.*

Brown Scale was stunned.

Flaking Scales dismissed him by tipping her beak. The juveniles clucked in celebration. When Brown Scale rejoined them they needled him good naturedly with their beaks. A feeling of unity returned to the Flock.

As I have always said, Yellow Claws gushed to Flaking Scales, *we will never be as wise as you.*

All we have to do, the grand matriarch added, *is to be sure he does not mate when he reaches breeding age.*

Why? Yellow Claws asked. *I want my females to breed with him. I want descendants with thick, pebble-proof skin and keen intelligence.*

Can you be sure your descendants will inherit his good traits? Flaking Scales warned her. *He is deformed. Deformity breeds more deformity. Don't risk it.*

Yellow Claws, as always, bowed to her advice.

So I have to put up with him for the rest of my life, White Sail said, disappointed with Flaking Scales decision. *What if an opportunity to kill him presents itself, do we take it?*

Flaking Scales looked White Sail in the eyes. *My decision is final. Leave him alone.* With a harsh hiss, she dismissed the matriarchs from her hilltop.

6

The ID Shindo had shown to the woman who was collecting admissions for the university's Dino Days event was accurate. It just wasn't specific. It made him appear to be a nondescript government employee of the Ministry of Defense when he was in fact a secret agent.

Kaiju have been an increasing threat to national security, so much so that they were cutting into his lifestyle of car chases and beautiful women. He was currently in the role of a liaison officer with the naval base on Chichijima. His job was to be a middle man, collecting data from the base via a secure email server, compiling the data into a report, and then forwarding the report to his superiors. The assignment effectively anchored him to his desk.

After his talk with Professor Abe, Shindo took a cab back to Intelligence HQ. Sueko Hitomi, the new receptionist, greeted him with an effusive smile. She was single and the sparkle in her eyes never let Shindo forget it.

He showed her his proper ID. She in turn logged in his arrival.

"You have been in town quite a bit lately," Sueko said, noting his log entries.

"Technically, I'm still doing field work. It's just that I don't have to go out into the field to do the work."

"I'd ask what the job is but then you'd have to kill me if you told me."

"Quite right. You learn fast." Shindo gave her a smile, making sure it was platonic so she did not get the wrong idea. He never dated the staff. Company policy.

Shindo showed his ID a second time at the security checkpoint. Here it was all business as the stern-faced guard verified his identity and disabled the lock to the secure door. Passing through the door, he took the lift to the thirty-fifth floor. His partner Yomo Kuta spotted him in the hall.

"Hey, Shindo! You're back." Yomo caught up with him. He had a donut in his hand and powdered sugar on the front of his shirt. "So what's the verdict? Is the brown pterodactyl a new species or the same one?"

"Same one."

"Hah! I won a thousand yen."

"You did?"

"Yeah. The whole floor set up an office pool on whether or not the pterodactyl was a new monster."

"Don't you guys have anything better to do?" Shindo marched into his office.

Yomo followed him.

"The Chief wasn't in on it was he?" Shindo asked as he took off his jacket and hung it up on the coatrack by the door.

"Are you kidding?" Yomo peeked out in the hall and quickly closed the door. "Do you know what he'd say if he found out?"

"Yes, the same thing I am going to say." Shindo unstrapped his sidearm from his chest and hung it up by his jacket. "This is serious business. You're lucky I won't tell the taxpayers of how you're trivializing a security matter."

"All right! All right!" Yomo took another bite out of his donut and pulled up a chair. "So what's so serious about this little fella." He tapped Shindo's copy of Brown Scale's photo which was lying on the desk.

Shindo sat down and explained. "If he had been a new species then he would be a one-off. We wouldn't have to worry about him breeding a second generation. But the Professor says he's the same species, so we do have to worry. This creature is impervious to assault rifles now. Can you imagine what he is going to be like when he's grown up? Our laser cannons won't be able to stop him."

Yomo sobered up. "I see what you mean."

"Go collect your winnings. I'd like to get my report submitted. Do you want to do lunch?"

"Sure."

"Dhaba's?"

"Dhaba's would be great."

Yomo bowed out of the office so Shindo could get to work.

In an hour the report was written. He printed off seven copies and gave them to the courier to be delivered to their interested parties, one of whom was his boss, Goro Yamashita.

The clock struck twelve noon. Shindo met Yomo at the reception desk. Sueko told them to enjoy their lunch as they said their goodbyes to her.

Dhaba's served the best salted mint lassi outside of India. Lassi was something of a yogurt smoothie. The mint leaves added the magic touch that helped Shindo feel refreshed while enduring the sweatbox heat of Tokyo's summer days. Yomo settled with iced coffee. They ordered two plates of curry and rice, Shindo's treat.

After lunch, Shindo sat in his office and waited. Goro was a fast reader, so the phone should ring right about...he checked his watch...now.

And then the phone rang. He answered the call.

"Shindo here."

"Get into my office right away." It was Goro.

"Is it about my report?"

"Yes."

Shindo hung up the phone.

Goro told him to sit down without so much as a hello when he stepped into the office. Shindo shut the door and took a seat.

Goro Yamashita was a stocky man with large hands that could pound the desk with the force of a sledge hammer. His voice could hit a person's ears with the same impact. To be fair, Goro Yamashita was not all rage and fury. He was more tolerant of Shindo than he should be. Shindo recognized that. Goro was a secret agent himself in his youth, and rumor had it he was a bigger pain in the rear to his chief than Shindo was to him. They were chips off the same block. Willful and independent, with too much respect for the job and not enough left over for the boss. This was the unspoken understanding between them. Nevertheless, Goro should never be trifled with.

"I read your report," Goro announced.

"I noticed." Shindo glanced down at his work. His report with the photos of the brown kaiju pterosaur lay spread out across the desk like incriminating evidence.

"I also read your recommendation."

"And that's why I'm here."

Goro locked eyes with him to be sure he was listening carefully. "When I assigned you as the liaison officer with the naval base on Chichijima what were my instructions regarding recommendations?"

"I was to run them by you first."

"Correct. Why did you fail to do so?"

"Let's get to the point, do you disagree with my recommendation?"

Goro scowled at him. His thick lips pressed into a thin, hard line. After a moment of reflection he relaxed. "No, I don't disagree. But that does not excuse you from disobeying my directives."

"And if I had aired my recommendation to you, would you have allowed me to include them in my report?"

"No."

"And that's why I didn't clear my recommendation with you first."

Shindo's blunt insubordination caused Goro to flinch as though someone had just kicked his chair.

Goro slapped the desktop and shook his head, unsure of what to do with his wayward son, metaphorically speaking. He sighed and tried again to get Shindo to see the big picture.

"It's bad enough when you dress up this little brown pterosaur to look like a bigger threat than Tiamatodon, but when you get a high caliber name like Professor Yuzo Abe to rubberstamp your recommendation, you put the prime minister in a position where he has to call his advisors together to evaluate your recommendation's merit. A lot rides on these decisions. The prime minister promised the public in the last election that he can protect us from the kaiju. He has to follow through on his promise and if he prioritizes the wrong monster, he will lose face. But, if the wrong monster happens to be our monster, then he can save face by blaming us. That's why I never involve myself in these decisions.

"The best thing to do is pass on the information you've collected from the navy and let the prime minister and his advisors decide what the priorities should be."

Shindo paused to show he was taking every word seriously. "What if I were to tell you that I was so confident in my assessment that I am willing to put my career at risk."

"Are you?"

"I am."

"Good," Goro nodded in satisfaction, "because I just got off the phone with the prime minister's secretary ten minutes ago. He called a meeting at The Château regarding your report and you are going with me to justify your recommendation. If I were you, I'd bring your professor along. You'll need him."

7

Shindo flew out to Hokkaido via helicopter. Professor Abe sat across from him in the passenger compartment. The professor glanced out the window and muttered in amazement at what he saw. Trees covered the entire landscape. It looked more like they were flying over the American northwest than Japan. There was not a skyscraper in sight. They passed over a gorge where a waterfall spilled white, foaming water into the stream below. The engine revved as the helicopter rose up and over the next rise. An isolated building could be barely seen amongst the dense foliage. No roads lead to this place. Not even a hiking trail.

"That's it," Shindo announced. "The Château."

"Looks like a haunted resort," Abe observed.

The helicopter settled on the helipad further down the slope.

Abe hung onto his hat as they hopped out. The helicopter took off.

A guard dressed as a forest ranger checked their IDs and allowed them to proceed into the cave where they passed a guard house staffed by several more soldiers dressed as forest rangers. One stepped out with a smile.

"Welcome back, Yamaguchi-san. I'll let you in."

The soldier pressed the button to release the lock and swung open the armor-plated door.

Shindo led Abe through a tunnel. After passing through another checkpoint they entered the lower levels of the structure they had seen from the air. Shindo forgot about the exclusive attitude of The Château's personnel. Everyone greeted him by name while they treated Abe as though he were invisible. In return the professor gave them guarded looks. Then one of the wait staff stopped them in the hall.

"Professor Yuzo Abe, I heard you were coming. Would you sign your book? It's for my son."

Abe perked up. "Why, yes! Of course. Let's see which one you got there." He read the title. "*Mammal-like Reptiles, the Lords of the Permian Period.* Heh-heh! I got a lot of satisfaction out of writing this book. Most people think the animals that lived prior to the Age of the Dinosaurs are boring. They completely overlook the diversification that sprouted at the end of the Paleozoic. And by most people, I refer to my colleagues."

After he signed the inside cover he returned the book.

The staffer accepted it with a bow.

From then on Abe felt more at home.

Shindo showed him to his room. The amenities would rate five stars if this were in a hotel.

Abe whistled. "I am going to be spoiled after this."

Shindo gave him a rundown on the thermostat, bathroom's location, and the phone for ordering room service.

"I take it there is no outside line," Abe remarked.

"No. No outside lines. No internet access. No outgoing mail. But you do have a TV." Shindo pointed at the 64-inch flat screen on the wall.

"Which plays propaganda reels around the clock."

Shindo laughed. "No, it's regular television." He switched on the set with the remote to prove his point.

"Don't you think this bunker in the woods is a waste of taxpayer money?" Abe plopped his suitcase on the couch and set his hat on top. "Can't the prime minister iron out his kaiju policy in Tokyo?"

"Absolutely." Shindo switched off the TV. "But Tokyo is infested with spies. Every time a kaiju damages our laser cannons there is a race with foreign powers to recover the wreckage. The prime minister holds his meetings here so the intelligence agencies of other countries don't find out where those cannons are deployed. That technology is reserved for use against kaiju. We don't want those guns starting a whole new arms race."

Shindo left him so he could freshen up for the big meeting. He found his chief Goro Yamashita in the lounge along with Yomo and Sayoko, Yomo's wife. Her beauty reminded Shindo of the glamourous actresses who graced Japanese cinema back in its peak in the 1960s. Her pale complexion was the only thing that betrayed the fact that she headed the R&D department at Mushita Electronics. Sayoko didn't get much sun working in a dust-proof lab.

Akira Ifukube's *Chant de la sérinde* played softly over the room's speakers. Its tranquil notes blended well with the view of the forest outside.

A waiter in tails brought drinks on a silver platter.

"How is the professor enjoying his first day at The Château?" Goro asked.

"I don't think he likes being cut off from the rest of the world," Shindo remarked. "It's a bit like jury duty to him."

"This is an important meeting for my company," Sayoko said.

"Oh?" Shindo was intrigued.

"We developed a new laser cannon, the Type VII *Heartbreaker*. The Type VI is hot enough to drive kaiju off our shores. With the Type VII we hope to finally be able to puncture their tough skin. The proto type is ready to be put into action. We designed it as a deterrent against Tiamatodon, but if you change the prime minister's mind, your brown monster will be its first target."

"How would you deploy it? Flocks inhabit islands."

"The Type VII is about the same size as the 127mm gun carried by our destroyers. Just swap turrets and then clear out the gun's magazine to make room for the laser cannon's generator and then you're set to go." Sayoko shrugged. "It would take no more than four hours to complete the conversion."

"Do you think you will be able to convince the prime minister to make your monster his top priority?" Yomo asked Shindo.

"General Umezo is a Tiamatodon fanatic," Goro noted.

"All of the prime minister's advisors are Tiamatodon fanatics," Shindo said. "I don't think in terms of whether or not if I can do it. I think in terms of should it be done, and yes, this needs to be done."

After dinner, the prime minister held audience in a conference room down in the reinforced concrete bowels of The Château. His advisors sat on either side of him. The medals and bars on their uniforms were proof of their experience. Shindo had no medals. His black suit, tie, and government credentials impressed civilians, but to these military men, working in intelligence amounted to no more than running errands.

Shindo could tell the prime minister's advisors already had their minds made up.

He presented footage from the *Sakai-maru's* onboard cameras. Led by the armored juvenile, the Flock offspring whipped around the rock outcroppings, flying low over the waves. The ship's forward batteries lowered their guns as far as they could, but the deck blocked their line of sight. Shindo noted the frowns on the faces of the prime minister's advisors. For a moment the juveniles vanished from sight and then suddenly appeared along the ship's flanks.

The brown one grabbed the CIWS 20mm rotary cannon, exerted force on it for a moment and then released it with a squawk. The juvenile looked as though he were trying to force the rotary cannon to fire at the gun turret.

General Umezo glanced toward the prime minister to gauge his reaction.

Footage from a different camera showed sailors from atop the bridge firing down at the brown creature and his two white-skinned sisters. The bullets from their assault rifles could be seen bouncing off the armored juvenile. It cawed to its sisters who got behind him and then flapped up to the top of the bridge. When they reached the top, the two sisters sprung out and attacked the crew.

Following the skirmish atop the bridge, the footage jumped to the armored juvenile aiming the assault rifle at the ship's crew, not once, but twice. Shindo paused the film at the moment the juvenile aimed the assault rifle for a second time. He then added a photo of the juvenile trying to push the rotary cannon toward the gun turret, forcing the prime minister and his advisors to look at the two instances where the armored juvenile tried to use the ship's weapons against the crew.

"This is a disturbing sight," Shindo jutted his thumb at the frozen images, "but let's address your arguments on why this shouldn't be a concern. This creature didn't figure out how to use the gun and even if he did an assault rifle is incomparable to Tiamatodon's destructive power. The rifle can punch out a window while Tiamatodon's plasma rays level entire city blocks. Therefore, the armored Flock juvenile is not a clear and present danger—today.

"Eventually Tiamatodon is going to grow old and die while this armored juvenile, if allowed to reach maturity, could pass his traits onto the next generation of Flock pterosaurs, traits that will not only make them immune to our guns but smart enough to turn our guns against us. These traits are like a virus that needs to be stamped out before it spreads.

"Biology is not my strong suite," Shindo said in conclusion, "so I've asked Professor Yuzo Abe of Momokita University to give you a clearer picture of what we are facing."

Professor Abe took Shindo's place at the lectern. The prime minister led the room in applause out of respect to their guest speaker.

Shindo sat down beside Goro.

Professor Abe thanked the audience for the kind reception.

"Mr. Yamaguchi is correct. This is evolution in action." Abe held his hand out to the freeze-frame image of the armored juvenile. "There has always been an arms race between predator and prey. The race waged by the dinosaurs was especially dynamic."

The professor took the pointer that was inside the lectern and put illustrations of two slender dinosaurs on the projection screen.

"*Coelophysis*." He tapped the dinosaur on the left. "A predator, 2.7 meters long."

"*Saturnalia.*" He tapped the dinosaur on the right. "An herbivore, 1.5 meters long. Rather similar in appearance, aren't they? Bipedal, gracile limbs, long necks, small heads, small size. The only significant difference is their diet. Both animals lived during the Carnian stage of the Triassic period. This is the starting gate of the arms race. This is where it began." He tapped the screen for emphasis.

"This is where it ended." Professor Abe replaced the images of *Coelophysis* and *Saturnalia* with illustrations of *Tyrannosaurus rex*, a *Triceratops*, and an *Ankylosaurus*. "Tyrannosaur teeth had a D-shaped cross section, unlike *Allosaurus*, *Carcharodontosaurus*, and other carnivorous theropods. Those animals had laterally compressed teeth, which were ideal for ripping meat. *Tyrannosaurus*' teeth crushed bones. It is little wonder the herbivores evolved an array of weaponry to protect themselves against this eating machine." He circled the *Tyrannosaurus* with the pointer. "Look at the horns atop the head of the *Triceratops* and the frill protecting his neck. He is like a gladiator with a sword and shield. Now look at *Ankylosaurus*. He is like a knight. Dermal armor cover his head, back, and flanks. His tail wields a bony club. These gentle giants were equipped to do battle.

"The Flock pterosaurs are not dinosaurs but their lineage shared a common ancestor with the dinosaurs. It's clear the Flock pterosaurs also share the same spirit of adaptation. Nature equipped us with an advanced intellect and toolmaking abilities. These abilities allowed us to become the dominant animal on the planet. But Nature has not forsaken her other children. We are in an arms race against the Flock. If the armored juvenile lives long enough to sire offspring, his descendants could produce even more dramatic adaptations."

General Umezo raised his hand.

Professor Abe motioned to him to go ahead and speak.

"The Flock raid the coastlines. They don't go inland. Let's say the Flock produces bulletproof babies which grow up to be tank-proof adults. So what? When Tiamatodon comes ashore he does not stop at the coast. I can list the cities he has destroyed but I trust you read the headlines."

Shindo raised his hand to interject. "Consider this, General. Once the Flock offspring are bulletproof, they may not stop at the coast. The adults could start nesting in populated areas. If they're armor protects them from our weapons, how are we going to stop them?"

The general harrumphed. "If, if, if. Listen to what you're saying, Mr. Yamaguchi. You're weighing what might happen against what we know will happen."

The prime minister raised his hands for silence. When Shindo and the general quieted down, he asked Professor Abe to continue.

The professor thanked him and said, "The only other thing I want to bring to your attention is the growth rate of a Flock pterosaur." He put a chart up on the screen. The horizontal axes measured time ranging from zero to five months. The vertical axes measured height from zero to sixty-five meters. "Flock offspring are about a meter and a half in height at birth. They grow at a slow rate for the first three months." He traced a slowly rising red line on the chart. "Then after the third month the offspring experiences a growth spurt, gaining ten meters each week until it reaches fifty meters at the end of the fourth month." His pointer traced the exponential curve in the line. "At the top of this steep rise it reaches sexual maturity.

"Judging by the photos from the *Sakai-maru*, I'd say the armored juvenile is right here on the chart, at about two and a half meters." Abe poked the three month mark where the line was about to go into its steep rise. "You have one month before it reaches breeding age, Prime Minister. One month, and then we will find out if there is any truth to Mr. Yamaguchi's fears."

The prime minister excused everyone from the conference room so he could discuss his options with his advisors. While Shindo waited, he spent his time soaking in The Château's hot spring spa in the afternoon and dining with Yomo and Sayoko at night. Sayoko pestered him with the same topic she always did when the three of them were together. It unfolded like clockwork:

"Why haven't you settled down?"

"My line of work does not allow me the time."

"Yomo is in the same line of work and he found the time." Sayoko paused at this point to squeeze her husband's hand and smile invitingly at him. Yomo then kissed her.

"Yomo is a multifaceted man. I'm not."

"Well, I'm getting tired of being the only girl at the table."

Shindo let her have her moment to pout and then changed the subject. Of course she didn't pout for real. It was more of a motherly kick in the pants to do what she thought was best for him, with the added benefit that she would have a woman to speak to when they got together.

The following day Shindo and his two friends took a hike through the woods with several armed guards. Bears were in abundance in the Hokkaido wilderness.

Professor Abe spent his time in his room reading. The Château featured a two-thousand volume library of which a hundred sixteen books filled their section on natural history. Shindo didn't anticipate seeing Abe any time soon during their stay.

At the end of the second day Goro Yamashita stopped at Shindo's room to give him the news. The prime minister had finalized his decision.

"The armored juvenile is taking priority over Tiamatodon."

Shindo exhaled with relief. "What changed his mind?"

"I told the defense minister the question is not which monster should take priority. The question is do we want a future where we have to fight both Tiamatodon and armored Flock pterosaurs? That raised his brows. He talked to the prime minister. Two hours later he phoned me and gave me the good news. The prime minister wants to stamp out the brown monster before the Flock problem can get worse. Now the bad news."

"Bad news?"

"Yes. Sayoko's new laser cannon will be mounted to a destroyer docked at the Chichijima naval base. That ship will head south with its own flotilla to join the *Sakai-maru* and her escorts."

"Sounds good so far. What's the bad news?"

Goro took a breath first before continuing. "We need security aboard the destroyer to be sure no one except for Mushita's personnel has access to the laser cannon. The prime minister decided that it was best that a person from the secret service handle that job. General Umezo recommended you. After all, you were the one who cited the armored juvenile as a threat to national security. Therefore you should see this mission through to its conclusion.

"What I don't like is that there is a good chance Tiamatodon will find you before you find the Flock. And if that happens you won't be coming back. I should have followed my own advice and shut up. You're my best man, Shindo. I hate to risk you over a job that can be done just as well by a field agent with less experience."

Something struck Shindo as suspicious. "Give me your honest opinion. If the prime minister had decided to go after the armored juvenile on his own, without any input from me, do you think General Umezo would have recommended that I go along with the task force?"

Goro carefully considered what would have been the likely outcome. "Probably not."

"I didn't think so either."

Part 2

8

Shindo returned to his home in Tokyo and packed for his flight to Chichijima. He met Yomo and Sayoko at the airport terminal. Goro assigned Yomo to this mission as a second pair of eyes would be needed to watch the gun. To Shindo's surprise Sayoko was coming along. Her boss, Kenzo Mushita, wasn't keen on letting her go, but she insisted since she understood the Type VII *Heartbreaker* laser cannon better than anyone, and Mushita Electronics could not afford a glitch in its operation. The Japanese government would likely cancel their order for subsequent Type VIIs if anything went wrong and with the gun being exposed to the corrosive effects of sea air, the possibility of something going wrong was substantial.

They flew down to Chichijima. Chichijima, which meant "Father Island" in English, was the northern most island in the Ogasawara archipelago. It was a thousand kilometers south of Tokyo. From the air it looked like a worn out green carpet thrown over a pile of rocks. An unbroken swath of shrubs covered its rugged terrain. Aside from the bustling harbor there appeared to be little habitation.

The Japanese SDF flew the parts of the cannon to Chichijima on a separate aircraft. From the airfield the SDF trucked the parts to the dry dock where the cannon was mounted to the *Kaga-maru*, a *Takanami*-class destroyer. It took four hours to replace the 127mm gun with the laser cannon, just as Sayoko said it would, however tests needed to be conducted to be sure the cannon's systems worked.

While they waited, the *Kaga-maru's* commander, Captain Ibō Takagi, gave Shindo and

Yomo a tour of his ship. Ibō Takagi was a strikingly handsome young man of twenty-eight years and he had the maturity of a person twice his age. Shindo could tell by his demeanor he had a flair for diplomacy as well. Perhaps he got it from his father, who was a member of the House of Councilors. Shindo could also tell by the small talk Captain Takagi engaged in that the captain was using the tour to gauge what kind of men he and Yomo were.

The following morning the ship set sail with three frigates, a replenishment oiler and a research vessel. The government released no announcement of their mission to the public, although Tokyo did notify the United Nations Security Council of the *Kaga-maru's* deployment.

Shindo donned a uniform which was identical to a naval officer's. His name tag said "S. Yamaguchi" in English letters. Below the nametag on his chest was a badge with the Defense Ministry's emblem. Yomo wore the same uniform with a name tag that read "Y. Kuta". Both of them had a high-caliber handgun strapped to their hip to show that they meant business.

They took turns watching the Type VII laser cannon. One day Yomo would be standing watch at the turret while Shindo would be down below guarding the generator. Then they swapped posts the following day. The ship's crew was too preoccupied to be a problem and when Shindo did encounter them they were polite and cooperative. He spoke more often with the personnel from Mushita Electronics. The job became a humdrum exercise in procedure. The Mushita people showed their ID. Shindo verified their identification. He said, "Good morning." They said, "Good morning." He asked, "How are you?" They said, "Fine. How are you?" He said, "Doing well," and then allowed them access.

Meals could be politely described as utilitarian. They were nutritious but bland and lean on portions. Yomo quipped that he had no complaints. He could stand to lose a few pounds.

Shindo didn't comment. He just smiled and wiped his mouth with his napkin.

After a week at sea, Captain Takagi invited Shindo, Yomo and Sayoko to the officer's mess for a steak dinner and a glass of wine. The meat was perfect—a cut of Grade A5 Wagyu beef—and its preparation was equal to its quality.

"I imagine it must feel good to eat like a civilian again," the captain observed, topping off everyone's wine glass.

"Heavenly," Sayoko sighed.

"Savor it," Shindo advised her. "We probably won't have food like this until we get back to Tokyo."

"Mr. Yamaguchi," Captain Takagi slid his empty plate back so he had room to set his elbows on the table, "how much bigger do you think the armored juvenile has grown since we had set sail?"

"Professor Abe said that the juvenile would be starting its growth spurt soon. That was nine days ago. If it hasn't started its growth spurt by now, then it should any day."

"And then?"

"And then it gains ten meters in height each week until it reaches fifty meters. At fifty meters it reaches sexual maturity. The good news is its growth rate slows back down. The bad news is that it can start breeding and when it does we could face a whole new generation of Flock pterosaurs that are just like him."

"Hm." Captain Takagi became thoughtful for a moment. "Then the race is on. Tomorrow morning we will be crossing the equator and entering the South Pacific. The South Pacific is like the Old American

West. It is a wide open frontier with a few military outposts and small towns. In the Old West you had to watch out for scorpions, rattlesnakes, and outlaws. In the South Pacific we will have to watch out for kaiju. This is their country. The *Sakai-maru* is already out there on her own with two frigates and an oiler. There's no guarantee that we will link up, but I can guarantee this much. Expect the next four weeks to be like war— long days of boredom interrupted by moments of terror."

9

Razor Beak and Peeps recovered from their injuries and were stronger than ever before. They didn't even have any scars. Their mother told them that they had entered their growth spurt. A wound taken in the morning would be healed by nightfall. That was what they could expect as their young bodies raced toward adulthood. Yellow Claws' offspring had not reached the growth spurt stage and it was noticeable. Their recovery rate lagged behind White Sail's offspring, although Flaking Scales deemed both broods fit enough for a second raid.

Flaking Scales sent the Gray Sisters in search of another target. They found an island populated by humans. The humans were armed but not as well armed as the ones manning the machine the juveniles had attacked in their first raid. The Gray Sisters felt the tingle of invisible waves that the humans used to see over long distances coming from the island. They located the device that emitted the waves, destroyed it, and returned to report their finding to Flaking Scales.

Flaking Scales ordered White Sail and Yellow Claws to take their broods out within the hour so they could arrive before nightfall. The grand matriarch advised the juveniles to attack with the sun at their backs. That way the humans would have the sun in their eyes when they fired their pebble shooters.

Brown Scale ruminated over whether or not he would be able to use a pebble shooter. During the raid on the seagoing machine, he was a half meter larger than a human. He had grown to twice the size of a human since.

The island appeared on the horizon. According to the Gray Sisters' memories the island resembled a turtle's head with an open mouth. The mouth formed a harbor. An ancient volcano stood where the eye would be. Palm trees covered the rest of the island. A beach of white sand ringed three-quarters of the island.

White Sail asked via telepathy if anyone felt a tingling sensation.

No one did.

The Gray Sisters said no one should. They had dropped the wave-emitting device into the sea. Unless the humans had a spare, they should be able to take the humans by surprise.

The black cone of the dead volcano stood out in stark relief against the clear blue sky as they drew closer. The sun had passed its zenith and was starting its slow descent. The two mothers turned westward, circling around the island, and then flew higher into the sky where the air was cold and the wind whistled in the ears. Once there, they glided in circles. When the offspring caught up, the two mothers ordered them to attack.

The Gray Sisters led the charge. A siren screamed. Humans scurried like insects. The Sisters dove for the harbor, drawing fire from the smoke puffers, allowing the juveniles to attack with impunity. Brown Scale attacked the humans that were firing one of the double-barreled smoke puffers. The puffer sat in a concrete pit located at the mouth of the harbor. Brown Scale shredded the ammo carrier with his claws, snapped the loader's neck, and yanked the gunner from his seat. Razor Beak, Peeps, and their unnamed brother pounced on the humans who were going to attack Brown Scale with their pebble shooters. The remaining humans in the area fled.

A big smoke puffer boomed from the far side of the harbor. Its shell exploded close by, pelting Brown Scale and his siblings with metal fragments. The same type of big puffer was on their side of the harbor.

Fly behind the smoke puffer, he said to Razor Beak via telepathy, *and show me how the humans are using it.*

Razor Beak acknowledged him with a caw and flapped to the other side of the harbor.

Brown Scale, Peeps, and their brother shuffled over to the big puffer. It too sat in a cement pit with the barrel poking over the parapet. Soon Razor Beak was telepathically showing Brown Scale what she could see of the humans firing the puffer. Brown Scale located the wheels and levers on the gun and then searched for the ammunition, all the while the puffer on the other side of the harbor was taking potshots at them.

Peeps peeped that they should leave. The fragments from the explosions were sharp and the explosions' roar frightened her.

Their brother agreed.

Brown Scale ordered his brother to grab a wheel on the side of the gun and spin it.

His brother did so, with difficulty as he had no thumb.

Brown Scale told him to stop when the puffer pointed at the other puffer on the opposite side of the harbor. He pulled a lever, opening the breech. Then he rolled a brightly colored metallic object over to the gun, picked it up with his beak and stuffed it into the breech. Closing the breech, he told his brother to spin a second wheel, lowering the puffer barrel. With a caw, he told his brother to stop and then with his thumb he pressed the magic spot that caused the puffer to go boom.

The puffer barked, kicking up dust all around the pit.

Its shell arced across the harbor and exploded in front of the enemy puffer. Dirt spewed like a geyser into the air.

Brown Scale's siblings cawed in joy.

Razor Beak telepathically showed Brown Scale how the humans reacted in shock.

Brown Scale told his brother to spin the wheel in the opposite direction, raising the barrel. After increasing the elevation a couple of degrees, Brown Scale told him to stop and stuffed a second bright metallic object into the breech, pressed the magic spot, and their puffer barked again.

The second shot exploded beside the enemy puffer. Several humans flew up into the air with the dirt and plopped outside their pit. The tattered bodies lay still.

The rest of the humans abandoned their gun.

Peeps and their unnamed brother celebrated with more cawing.

Then a shadow descended upon Brown Scale and his siblings. The ground shook as a mountain of rage dropped outside the pit. It was their mother.

You are supposed to be learning how to fight, White Sail hissed savagely. *I did not bring you here so you can play!*

Terrified, Brown Scale, Peeps, and their brother scrambled back into the air.

The Gray Sisters were smashing the wooden buildings to force the humans who were hiding inside them to flee out into the open. Yellow Claws' offspring and Brown Scale's unnamed sister flew into them, striking the humans in the head with their sharp keels. To confuse the humans, they crisscrossed their flight paths. The humans had no idea which way to run. Dead bodies with cracked skulls littered the ground by the time Brown Scale and his siblings caught up with the other juveniles.

Seeing how well Yellow Claws' brood had everything under control, Brown Scale and his siblings headed for another set of buildings tucked in the palm grove. These were long with large openings on the end. Boxes like the ones stacked aboard the ships in the harbor were piled high inside and outside the buildings.

The humans in this area were armed with pebble shooters and wore olive-colored outer skins.

Brown Scale led the attack, drawing fire. He struck the closest human with his keel. Its head cracked like a coconut. A wet, coppery smell erupted from the strike. His brother and Razor Beak each achieved a kill as they followed him in their pursuit of the armed humans.

However, the narrow rows of boxes forced them to land. A human popped out of hiding and fired at Brown Scale. The pebbles bounced off his armored chest. He quickly grabbed the human with his beak and snapped his neck before the creature could shoot pebbles at his siblings.

Four more armed humans leapt from ambush points amongst the boxes.

Brown Scale's brother grabbed the pebble shooter from the dead human and held it out toward the dead human's comrades. The humans cowered at first but when they saw that the unnamed brother was holding the shooter sidewise instead of pointing it at them, they regained their courage and riddled Brown Scale's brother with pebbles. One of the pebble shooters was larger than the others and was especially fierce. Its pebbles cut deep into his brother's flesh. His blood splattered all over his white, fur-covered chest. He screeched as the stream of pebbles knocked him off his feet.

Brown Scale grabbed the shooter his brother dropped and pointed it at the humans. This time it worked. Fire belched from the shooter as its pebbles put holes into the nearest human. He staggered from the impact and then fell onto his back and didn't get up. Two of the other humans glanced down at their dead comrade and then ran. The one with the big shooter turned his weapon toward Brown Scale. Brown Scale fired first, cutting the human down.

Take our brother home, Brown Scale cawed to Razor Beak.

Razor Beak grabbed their bleeding brother with her feet and flew out of the battle zone.

Brown Scale picked up the big shooter. It was heavy with a box attached to the underside. It also had a spur like the smaller shooter. He figured out that this spur must be squeezed in order to make the pebbles come out of the stick. Squeezing the spur, he unleashed a stream of pebbles which ripped through the boxes and the humans hiding behind them. He proceeded into the rows of boxes with Peeps hissing at the humans over his shoulder. Any human that tried to attack him from the flanks, Peeps grabbed the creature with her beak and snapped his neck.

They emerged from the boxes and reached the buildings. The pebbles cut through the thin walls of the buildings. The humans had no place to take shelter. They ran in every direction, but the big pebble shooter had a long reach. Brown Scale could shoot pebbles across the open ground, striking buildings far away. One set of buildings spilled a foul-smelling liquid. It rapidly spread across the artificial ground. The humans screamed in panic. Brown Scale kept shooting at the buildings spilling liquid since it frightened the humans so much.

For reasons Brown Scale could not fathom the liquid burst into flames. The buildings containing the liquid blew their tops. Fire consumed the nearby buildings and humans.

Peeps cawed in awe.

Brown Scale stared in silence.

She nudged him with her beak to break him out of his reverie. The flaming liquid was spreading toward them.

Brown Scale put the big shooter into his mouth and they flew back to Yellow Claws' brood. The Gray Sisters stared at them as they passed, wondering what they did to cause such a commotion.

Yellow Claws' offspring landed to watch the conflagration rising over the treetops. They would fall prey to the humans if they stayed grounded for too long. The Gray Sisters cawed, telling them it was time to go home.

The offspring were happy to leave. Fighting humans was getting boring. They leapt back into the air and followed the Gray Sisters back to their mothers who were circling in the air off the coast of the island. Both broods returned home, arriving at their island after sunset.

White Sail and Yellow Claws reported to Flaking Scales what happened at the raid in the usual way, using memories. Flaking Scales was not happy with what she saw. She misjudged Brown Scale's intelligence. He wasted time playing with the smoke puffer. Worse yet, he preoccupied three of his siblings with the gun. They managed to kill two humans, but Yellow Claws' brood killed three dozen humans with their keels. If Brown Scale and his siblings had been helping at least another four dozen humans could have been added to the tally.

Yellow Claws reminded Flaking Scales that Brown Scale had killed a number of humans with a pebble shooter.

Flaking Scales then reminded her that he caused a fire with the shooter that nearly killed himself and Peeps. What if the other juveniles were present? He could have wiped out both broods!

Flaking Scales then called Razor Beak to the hilltop. When she came, Flaking Scales rebuked her with a sharp hiss. She should not have brought her injured brother home. She should have left him.

He would have died if she hadn't brought him back, White Sail protested through telepathy.

Flaking Scales stood her ground. *The raids separate the weak from the strong. The strong then produce healthy offspring when they reach breeding age. Your male is weak. He must die so he cannot weaken the bloodline with his seed.*

My unnamed son is my only viable male, White Sail replied. *I will not kill him.*

You are young, Flaking Scales reminded her. *You can give birth to another male.*

I will not kill him! White Sail broke the circle and flew back to her nest where her injured offspring lay panting from his wounds.

You did not mind that Brown Scale brought Pearly White to me, Yellow Claws telepathically said to the grand matriarch.

That was acceptable because Pearly White was going to die anyway, Flaking Scales replied. *Her weakness was not going to pollute the bloodline. White Sail's son will live and it will be to the determent of the next generation.*

Flushed with emotion, Yellow Claws blurted out a sharp, angry squawk and left the hilltop.

A growl rumbled in Flaking Scales throat. She looked down at tiny Razor Beak and spoke to her in a series of croaks and clucks. *Do not let sentiment control you or it will cloud your judgement, too. Listen to me and you will grow up to be wise.*

Razor Beak stared up at her without comment. When Flaking Scales finished her advice, the young female acknowledged her with a cluck and flew to her mother.

White Sail stroked Razor Beak with her beak in gratitude.

Razor Beak spoke to her with chirps and clucks. *Brown Scale told me to save him*, she said in regard to her unnamed brother.

That is what happened, the unnamed brother clucked. He panted, swallowed to wet his throat, and clucked some more. *Brown Scale saved me.*

After returning home from the raid, Brown Scale flew to his roost amongst the outcroppings on the coast to rest. He had brought the big shooter with him. During the raid on the seaborne machine he was able to wrap his thumb and three fingers around the shooter's handgrip. Today he was able to wrap a thumb and one finger around the grip. By the next raid he might not be able to hold a shooter at all.

He poked the gun with his beak, nudging it into a safe nook where wind and rain could not get at it.

The moon rose, blotting out many of the stars with its radiance.

Brown Scale tucked his head between his wings and closed his eyes to sleep.

The leathery flap of massive wings sounded outside his roost.

He opened his eyes to see his mother land outside his roost. She put a three-meter long squid at his feet.

White Sail looked at him with both eyes. Since his birth she only looked at him with her injured eye to remind him of what he had done to her.

Before he could react she flew away, leaving him with her peace offering.

Brown Scale ate the squid and slept well that night.

In the morning he took his pebble shooter to White Sail. His unnamed brother was lying in their old nest, sleeping fitfully. He had stopped bleeding, but it would be a while before he would be well enough to fly. Their mother stood watch over him lest Flaking Scales tried to cull him from the Flock.

Brown Scale set the pebble shooter before her as an offering.

White Sail looked at it, poked it, and then picked it up with the tip of her huge beak, careful not to snap it in half. She then flew over to the ridge and stuck the shooter into the ground as a totem to ward off predators, including humans.

10

The *Kaga-maru* spotted smoke on the horizon. Smoke from an erupting volcano tended to be a light ash color. This smoke was black, like the smoke from a burning building or a forest fire, which indicated there had to be an island in that direction even though there were no islands in that area according to the chart. Captain Takagi decided to investigate.

As his flotilla neared the smoke they found that there was indeed an island. It was about half the size of Chichijima. Two cargo ships floated listlessly in its harbor. A fire raged in the palm grove along the shore. Captain Takagi put his command on alert when he saw coastal batteries and anti-aircraft gun positions at the mouth of the harbor. The AA guns were pointed inland while the coastal guns, for some strange reason, were aimed at each other. Still, it was best to be cautious.

Shindo rushed to the bridge when the klaxon sounded. Sayoko arrived right after he did with the fire controls to the laser cannon tucked under her arm. She opened the controls on a specially installed pedestal and plugged them in so she could operate the cannon.

"What do you make of this?" the captain asked Shindo.

"Smugglers. Maybe even pirates."

"No, that." Takagi pointed at the coastal batteries and then handed Shindo his binoculars.

Shindo examined the guns. One had two dead bodies lying beside it. The other had none. A rival gang could have infiltrated the island, but they would have no hope of accomplishing anything. The island was too well armed. The US Navy could have caused this much damage, but they would still be here to clean up the mess. That left one other culprit.

Shindo returned the binoculars. "When the Flock attacked the *Sakai-maru*, the first thing the armored juvenile did was try to force the CIWS cannon to shoot at the forward gun turret. Looks like his M.O. to me."

"You don't think he operated one of those coastal guns, do you?"

"I suggest you send a landing party ashore to find out."

Shindo accompanied the landing party. They encountered no resistance from the pirates. Many of the people lingering on the docks were women and their children. Their faces were smudged with ash. They stared vacantly in a state of shellshock. The men were either battling the flames or watching the coasts for another attack. Several militia men in olive-colored uniforms and armed with Chinese manufactured assault rifles ran up to Takagi's men. The militia man with a sergeant's stripes on his sleeves spoke.

"Are you US Navy?" he asked in Spanish.

Fortunately Shindo could speak Spanish. "No, we're with the Japanese Maritime Self-Defense Force."

"Are you US Navy?" the militia man kept repeating.

"No, no, we're Japanese," Shindo assured him.

The militia men relaxed.

"Who are you people?" Shindo asked.

"We need medical supplies," the sergeant pleaded, "and a radio."

Shindo noticed the flag of the Gold Dragons hoisted at the top of the flag pole.

"Are you with the Gold Dragons?" Shindo asked.

The sergeant ignored the question and asked for medical supplies and a radio. "We have women and children. See? They need help. We can't stop fire."

The flag was proof enough. The Gold Dragons was the largest pirate organization in the world, and the most dangerous. It was founded by Jerome Vedasto. Shindo never met the man but he had spoken to people who had. Vedasto was a loud fellow who greeted people with a rib-crunching hug. This warm demeanor masked a keen mind, a ruthless heart, and an unquenchable thirst for wealth. His organization was becoming a nation onto itself. Back in Vedasto's hometown, people nicknamed him 'the Governor'. The intelligence agencies of the Pacific Rim nations knew the Gold Dragons were operating from an uncharted island. They just couldn't find it.

The Flock did.

Shindo interviewed the militia men to get the full story of what happened.

According to the pirate soldiers, two big gray monsters ripped the radar dish from its installation and flew away. Later in the day the two gray monsters returned with two huge white ones and a dozen little ones. One of the little ones was brown. The brown one commandeered a coastal gun with the help of three other white ones. The militia men took Shindo to the location. The weapon was a Vickers 6-inch breech loader, a leftover from the Second World War. Its crew was nowhere in sight. There were footprints of Flock juveniles outside the gun pit. Shindo looked down the barrel, noting how well aimed it was at the battery on the other side of the harbor. A shiver went up his spine when he imagined the creature he was hunting had stood where he was standing now.

"While the brown one was firing our gun," the sergeant said, "the two big gray ones smashed our town. Come, look."

The pirates had established an entire community on the island including the militia, an airstrip, hospital, and housing for the pirates' wives and children. Shindo was led to the island's red light district. The people who were sheltering in the brothel and tavern had run out into the open to escape being crushed only to be attacked by the little ones. Shindo saw dozens of bodies lying outside the leveled buildings. Their skulls had been split open. The Flock juveniles must had attacked the islanders with the sharp keels on their chests. That was a common tactic.

"What about the brown one?" Shindo asked. "Did it do anything else besides fire the breech loader?"

"A huge white monster chased the brown one and his friends out of the gun pit." The sergeant held his arms up high and spread them out to give a picture of how big the white Flock adult was. "The brown one and his friends attacked our warehouses. My men shot one of his friends but then an uninjured monster carried away the wounded one. The brown one grabbed a light machine gun and killed several of my men. That is the truth. It fired an LMG. That is how the fire got started. It hit our fuel depot. The bullets sparked a fire. The fire spread to the warehouse where we store our ammunition. Caused explosions. Many explosions. Rocked the whole island. Killed hundreds. There is no fire department here. We can't put out the flames. Will you help us?"

"Is Vedasto here?" Shindo asked.

The sergeant clammed up. He realized that his answer would determine how much help his people were going to receive. His answer could also get him in trouble with his boss.

"I don't know a Vedasto," he blurted out.

"You don't know Vedasto?" Shindo said with doubt in his voice.

"I don't know any Vedasto."

"How about the Governor? Do you know anyone by that name?"

"No."

"Are you sure?"

The sergeant pursed his lips, looked at his men, and then out to the women and children gathered out on the shore. He looked worried.

Shindo glanced over his shoulder at the civilians. Some of them might be the sergeant's family.

"You said you need help," Shindo prodded the man.

The sergeant got the hint. "He is not here."

"Who? Vedasto? The Governor?"

"He is not here," was all the sergeant would reveal.

Shindo put his hands on his hips. "Fine. Which way did the monsters come from?"

The sergeant pointed toward the west.

"Which way did they go when they left?"

The sergeant pointed toward the southeast.

"Which direction did the two big gray monsters come from before the attack?"

"The southeast."

"Which way did they go after they destroyed your radar dish?"

"The southeast."

Shindo was satisfied. He clapped the man on the shoulder. "I will get you some help."

As he turned to leave the sergeant grabbed him and looked Shindo hard in the eyes. "If you are going after them be careful. Those monsters don't fight like monsters. They fight like soldiers."

11

Excitement brewed amongst the Flock when the Gray Sisters reached adulthood. Doubling the number of breeding age females meant doubling the Flock's numbers, or at least the potential existed.

However, the Gray Sisters complicated the matter by showing no interest in Male. Male wasn't interested in them, either, but the Gray Sisters expressed their lack of interest first. That allowed Male to use their disinterest as an excuse for his disinterest.

Flaking Scales was displeased.

She called them to her hilltop and demanded that they breed through a series of raspy hisses.

The Gray Sisters stood their ground. Unless they could mate with someone who could sire offspring with armored plating, like Brown Scale, they did not want to mate at all. What would be the point? They did not want weaklings like Pearly White.

Flaking Scales could see their heart's desire. They wanted to wait until Brown Scale was an adult. The grand matriarch narrowed her eyes and communicated in thought.

You can mate with Brown Scale. While you wait for him to reach breeding age, one of you must mate with Male. The Flock must grow its numbers.

The Gray Sisters narrowed their eyes back at her in suspicion. They doubted she would allow them to mate with him since she believed Brown Scale would pollute the bloodline with deformities.

Flaking Scales let out a ferocious hiss, threatening to kill them if they disobeyed her.

The Gray Sisters shrank back. Flaking Scales was old, but she was twelve meters taller than they were. They could not beat her in a fight. Reluctantly, they complied.

Male sighed. Getting intimate with one of the Gray Sisters made him feel queasy. They were too eccentric for his tastes. Yet, he would do his duty.

Flaking Scales told the Gray Sisters to go make their nests and then called the rest of the Flock to her hill. She announced the big news that Male would be choosing one of the Gray Sisters as his mate. With a new batch of eggs on the way, there would not be enough room on the island. She ordered everyone to pair up and fly in different directions. Their mission was to find a larger island. The only direction she did not want them to go was back to their old island. The Two-Headed One had been there once. It could return there again.

White Sail told Peeps and her unnamed sister to fly with their unnamed brother. They flew due east.

Yellow Claws sent her three remaining offspring off as one group and then paired up with White Sail. Her offspring flew southeast while she and White Sail flew due south.

Brown Scale and Razor Beak flew due west. They both had grown to ten meters in height since the raid on the island. Going off on their own without the adults no longer felt daunting.

They glided across the sea. The sun began to set. Soon it would be low enough to shine in their eyes.

Razor Beak cawed, suggesting that they should try a different direction.

Brown Scale had a gut feeling that they should go a little further.

Let's keep going, he said telepathically.

Razor Beak didn't respond.

He tried again, speaking telepathically. *Let's keep going.*

When he still didn't get a reply, he lowered the sail on his head and glanced in her direction.

She lowered her sail and glanced back at him and cawed again. *Let's search in a different direction.*

Then Brown Scale remembered. Their mental faculties weakened when their numbers were few. Razor Beak could no longer use telepathy.

Yet, he still could. He thought he did, anyway. It was hard to tell.

Brown Scale cawed. *Let's keep going a little further.*

She acknowledged him with a soft cluck.

They flew into the sunset. Night came and the radiance of the stars filled the sky with their magic. Up ahead they could see mountains silhouetted against the firmament. They slowed down and as they neared they could hear the waves slap against the rocks. They flew through a gap amongst the steep sloops guarding the shoreline and discovered a valley shrouded in a phosphorescent mist.

Brown Scale felt at home here. The tall mountains would afford shelter from storms, predators, prying human eyes, anything a creature could imagine. Even after he reached adulthood, the mountains would still be tall enough to make him feel safe. There were also many cliffs where he could roost and stare over his domain, if this place were his home.

Out of curiosity he dipped into the milky haze and encountered dense vegetation. He had to land lest he broke a wing finger.

Razor Beak landed behind him and shuffled close by his side so they would not lose sight of each other. The air here was humid and warm as a blanket.

They explored a forest of tree-size horsetails, tree ferns, and club mosses that stood thirty meters in height. Their trunks had a scaly surface, like a reptile. Vines and cycads carpeted the understory. A giant millipede slithered out into the open and with the determination of a locomotive it scurried between them. Razor Beak tried to grab it but it disappeared under the dense vines.

She then became distracted by a juicy griffin fly. She locked her eyes on her target and her head flicked side to side as the insect buzzed over her head, just out of reach.

Brown Scale watched her in dismay. Her instincts controlled her.

He cawed, *Did you forget why we are here?*

She stared at him, wondering why he felt something was wrong, and then clucked that she hadn't.

Brown Scale continued exploring the island. Razor Beak followed behind him as though she were his pet rather than his sister. It was sad to see her lose her reason, but at least he was able to hold onto his. He could still focus on their mission.

The griffin fly Razor Beak had missed came back and buzzed around their heads. This time Brown Scale heard a sharp crack and the buzzing stopped. Razor Beak caught the bug. Its exoskeleton sounded tantalizingly crispy as she chomped on it. Its juices dribbled on the ground. Brown Scale's belly started gurgling. He imagined the insect's innards had a smooth texture and a mild but satisfying taste. Razor Beak swallowed the bug and wiped the roof of her mouth clean with her tongue.

Ignoring his appetite, Brown Scale continued. Razor Beak followed.

The forest thinned up ahead. A herd of sluggish creatures browsed on a menagerie of ferns and horsetails. They had small round heads and swollen, pig-like bodies and long, thick tails.

A stream trickled down the center of the valley. Brown Scale tracked it to a shallow pond. By then the fog had broken up, leaving them in darkness. They kept plodding through the water, carefully, making sure the ground was firm enough to hold them.

Then lightning flashed above the mountains. Thunder followed. Startled, Razor Beak unfurled her sail and cawed at the sky. A bright light appeared on the far shore of the pond. In the center of the light was a giant reptile-like creature. It had a massive sail on its back like a fish, yet the rest of its body resembled that of a lizard. Its mouth had sharp teeth poking out from under its scaly lip, yet it showed no intent of making a meal out of the two young pterosaurs. Instead it lounged upon a massive boulder with one forepaw lying atop the other.

Brown Scale approached the creature.

Razor Beak lingered where she was until she was convinced that there was no danger and then caught up with her brother.

They looked up at the sail-back inquisitively. The creature looked down at Brown Scale. He could feel its mind probing his, going through his memories.

You are called Brown Scale, the sail-back said, using telepathy. It looked down at Razor Beak and riffled through her memories. Razor Beak shrank back, hissing. Its mind probing enraged her.

Brown Scale stroked the underside of her beak with his to calm her.

I don't like this place, she clucked. *Let's leave.*

The sail-back did not feel threatened by her anger. He remained languid and spoke to Brown Scale through telepathy.

The island sent me to welcome you.

The island sent you? Brown Scale did not understand.

The island is alive. All land is alive. It creeps across the sea of lava, changing form so slowly we animals die long before we see a river change its course or a desert sweep across a plain.

The sail-back put images in Brown Scale's mind of all the land across the world coming together, breaking apart and then regrouping into new lands. As the lands joined, mountains popped up. The terrain changed from jungles to forests to steppes to deserts. Ice sheets steamrolled over the countryside and then melted away leaving behind a host of lakes and rivers. The process repeated in many combinations as the land changed configuration.

Where is the sea of lava? Brown Scale asked.

Underneath the land. You can't see it, but it is there.

How do you know?

The island told me.

Brown Scale didn't believe him. The sail-back must be insane.

I am not insane, the sail-back said in response to his thoughts. *Just very, very old. Do you want to stay with us?*

Yes! I feel at home here.

Good. The island likes you. It wants to be left alone. You want to be left alone. You two are kindred spirits. But, there is one condition. You must not mate.

I don't want to mate.

Brown Scale sensed that the sail-back was pleased with his answer. *I am going to fly back to my Flock and tell them about this place. They are looking for a new home.*

No, the sail-back reptile replied. *The island does not want any new animals displacing the ones it already has. That is why you must not mate. So long as you are the only one of your kind you will not upset the balance of nature.*

Then I won't be able to live here today. If I survive long enough to become an adult I will return.

When you are ready, we will be here.

The light vanished. The pond was hidden again in darkness.

Brown Scale climbed up on the shore and searched for the sail-back and could not find him. He couldn't even find the boulder. The shore was empty.

12

Shindo spread the map of the Pacific Ocean out on the table in the CIC and then briefed Captain Takagi, Yomo, and Sayoko on what intelligence had been gathered thus far.

"This is where our problem started," Shindo put his finger on the map, "seven kilometers southeast of Iwo Jima. An air traffic controller spotted Tiamatodon rising up to the ocean surface. The Maritime Self-Defense Force high command dispatched the *Sakai-maru* to track the monster's movements. The *Sakai* followed it for several weeks until her crew lost sight of it on sonar. Captain Inoue maintained course in hope of picking up the trail. He found an island here in this open body of water that's surrounded by Wake Island, the Marshals, Micronesia, and the Marianna's. It was here," Shindo tapped the location on the map, "that the brown Flock juvenile and his siblings attack Inoue's ship. He didn't pick them up on radar until they came around the island's mountains. And they didn't originate from the island because the Flock nests that had been found on this island had been destroyed by Tiamatodon. So they had flown there from another location, using the mountains to block the ship's radar.

"Yesterday we discovered an uncharted island occupied by the Gold Dragon pirates here, just south of the equator. The Flock left the island, heading southeast. Here's the problem." Shindo traced a straight line leading away from the island the Flock colony had inhabited and a line from the pirate island. The lines were parallel. "These lines should cross. However, the *Sakai-maru* detected two blips on its radar approaching from a more southerly direction. As soon as the blips were detected, the blips turned around and departed in the same direction. The pirates also detected two blips before they were attacked."

"The two blips are the same two Flock pterosaurs," Captain Takagi concluded.

"That's right," Shindo nodded. "They're acting as scouts. Now if we draw a line heading south from the *Sakai-maru* instead of southeast it intersects with the pirate island line down here between New Zealand and Chile."

"Sheesh!" Sayoko exclaimed.

"Yeah, that's a long ways," Shindo agreed.

"It's going to take ten days to reach the area," Captain Takagi said, "and then who knows how long to find the armored juvenile's home."

"We may get some help." Shindo straightened up from bending over the map. "I sent a request to my superiors for a satellite to be sent over the area."

"Good." Captain Takagi was relieved to hear it. "I will contact Captain Inoue and ask him to swing around…"

Before he could finish the intercom buzzed. Takagi answered it.

"Captain," his executive officer said over the intercom's speaker, "kaiju sighted, approaching fast."

Captain Takagi put his command on alert. Sayoko followed him to the bridge while Shindo and Yomo headed to the armory where they strapped on a helmet and life preserver. The armorer handed Shindo a light machine gun and an assault rifle to Yomo. Yomo slung the rifle to his back then grabbed two extra ammo boxes for Shindo's LMG. They ran out onto the deck with the security detail. Shindo and Yomo took a position near the laser cannon. Above them several sailors mounted a machine gun to the railing of the bridge wing.

A petty officer passed the word that the kaiju was following the ships at a distance of fifteen kilometers at a speed of fifty knots. The ships were sailing at twenty knots.

According to the drill, personnel engaged a kaiju only if it attempted to make physical contact with the ship or if its wake endangered the ship's operation. Kaiju didn't always attack. At times they escorted a vessel out of its territory. Sometimes they were just curious. Other times they just wanted to play, especially if they were juveniles. As comforting as that sounded, there still was the delicate task of figuring out the creature's intent. Misjudging the creature's motives resulted in loss of life and often loss of the ship.

"There it is!" the petty officer cried out. He stood on the helipad at the back of the ship, pointing toward the water.

"Is it Tiamatodon?" another seaman called out.

"No!"

"Thank goodness for that," Yomo muttered.

A mass slithered just below the surface. The *Haruo-maru*, one of the escort frigates, sailed parallel with Captain Takagi's ship a kilometer away. The mass came up between the two ships and kept pace with them. Shindo could see what it was.

"It's Tylogon." He pressed the stock of the LMG into his shoulder, getting ready to fire. "Expect a fight."

"Yes, a fight," Yomo corrected, "not a slaughter."

Tylogon enjoyed the same advantage as the brown Flock juvenile had by being below the deck of the ships. The main batteries could not be depressed low enough to engage him, which left it up to sailors with small arms to drive him away. This was the situation Sayoko's boss, Kenzo Mushita worried about.

102

The kaiju *Tylosaurus* could sink the ship before his laser cannon could get a chance to fire a shot.

For the moment Tylogon swam with the ships. The ships maintained speed and course. Slowing down or stopping would not improve their situation.

Shindo lowered his weapon to give his arms a rest.

Then Tylogon unfurled his dorsal fin and swam ahead of the ships. His fin sliced through the waves like a knife, circled around the *Haruo*, and returned to the same position between the destroyer and her escort.

Tylogon raised his head above the waves and spewed twin spouts of water and mucus from his nostrils. There was a mischievous glint in his eye. Once he cleared the fluid from his nasal passages he let out a hardy roar, bearing his teeth.

A primeval fear shook Shindo's nerve.

Tylogon snapped his jaws at the men lined up on the deck of the *Haruo*. He huffed and snorted and then snapped his teeth at the sailors lined up aboard the *Kaga*. His open maw left the men awestruck. A truck could drive down his throat.

Shindo and the seaman aimed their weapons.

The petty officer called out, "Steady! Hold your fire!"

Tylogon lunged at the destroyer.

"Open fire!"

While the petty officer shouted his order everyone squeezed their triggers. Antitank rockets whooshed over the waves and crashed into Tylogon's snout. Shindo aimed for the nostril. The LMG kicked in his grip. His rounds peppered the jawline, chipping the rock-hard scales. The sea monster was coming in too fast to hit a soft point. Just before Tylogon reached the ship he dived into the water. His massive tail flapped in the air, flung water at the ship. Shindo got caught in the spray. His uniform was soaked. The tail plunged below the waves. A wake spread like a shockwave and swept up the ship. Shindo braced himself against the railing. The ship rocked side to side like a toy in a bathtub.

Tense moments ticked one after the other. Questions raced through Shindo's mind. How far did Tylogon dive? Where will he surface? Underneath them? In front?

The petty office pressed his headset close to his ear so he could hear his orders from the bridge, then cried out to the security detail, "Everyone to the back of the ship!"

Shindo and Yomo followed the security detail to the helipad at the back of the ship.

The ship fired depth charges. The charges plopped in the water. Seconds later they exploded. Water erupted out of the ocean.

Tylogon broke the surface with a roar. He charged the destroyer. The men opened fire. "Forget the MGs!" Shindo shouted. "Everyone fire antitank rockets!" He tossed aside his firearm and grabbed a disposable rocket launcher from the nearest ammo carrier. Everyone followed his example, discarding their squad automatics. AT rockets punched Tylogon in the face. Torpedoes from the *Haruo* and *Nakajima* slammed into the monster's flanks. He snarled in annoyance and dived back underwater.

The sailors watched the sea and listened for orders. The petty officer, with cool professionalism, waited for instructions.

"Sonar found him," the officer yelled, "he's swimming ahead of us at a depth of 75 meters, speed: 55 knots."

Shindo and Yomo ran back to the laser turret.

Over his headset, Shindo heard the alarm in the petty officer's voice when he cried, "Tylogon is coming back up to the surface—in front of the *Haruo-maru*!"

No sooner he spoke Tylogon burst from the water and flopped onto the bow of the frigate. His weight flipped the ship up on end. He slid off the deck. The ship hung motionless with its aft up in the air. Its screws spun uselessly. The men on the deck clung to the railing. Then the ship fell, superstructure first. Forty-nine hundred tons of warship hit the waves with a resounding wallop. Sheets of water shot up into air, veiling the *Haruo* from sight. When the water settled the *Haruo* floated belly-up like a dead fish.

Tylogon burst from the water and flopped on top of the capsized frigate. Grunting with joy, he chewed on the hull. His teeth scarred the surface but failed to punch through. Even so, he was as happy as a puppy with a new toy.

The main battery from the frigate paralleling the *Haruo* pelted Tylogon. The kaiju tylosaur bore up to the pounding and kept chewing on the hull. Then the Type VII *Heartbreaker* lanced a searing beam of laser light at the beast. Its touch peeled away Tylogon's thick hide. Melted fat bubbled out of the opened wound followed by a generous gush of blood. Tylogon wailed. He tried to persevere but couldn't. Abandoning his prize, he dove into the water.

The security detail cheered.

The petty officer announced the depths Tylogon reached until the kaiju swam out of sonar's range. "The bridge has given us the all clear," he called out. "The ship is no longer on alert. Return to your posts."

The men cheered again and patted each other on the back.

Shindo and Yomo pulled off their headsets and went up to the bridge. Yomo hugged his wife.

"Successful test," Shindo commented to Sayoko.

She pulled away from her husband, smiling. "Indeed! When we find your brown Flock juvenile, I don't anticipate any trouble."

13

Brown Scale and Razor Beak returned to their home island before dawn. Razor Beak regained her intellect now that she was within proximity to her Flock mates. Brown Scale still did not feel any different.

Did my intelligence weaken when we were on our own? Brown Scale asked in thought.

I did not notice, Razor Beak replied in kind. *Did mine?*

Brown Scale hid his memory of what happened to her when they were on their own and replied, *I did not notice.*

He had suffered enough grief because his body was different from everyone else. He did not want to suffer more grief because his mind was different, too.

Did you like the island we found? Brown Scale asked.

No. The insects are juicy, but there is an invisible creature living there. I felt unwelcomed in its territory.

Bury your memory of the island. I will bury mine. Then we will tell Flaking Scales that we only found water. No land.

Razor Beak concurred with a chirp.

They hid their memories and flew to Flaking Scales' hilltop to find five other adults which were as shriveled and gigantic as she was. Brown Scale flew over to his father. Male was sitting near the Gray Sister he had chosen to be his mate. He perked up when he saw his son.

Who are the old ones? Brown Scale asked telepathically.

They are members of the original matriarchy, his father replied.

Original matriarchy?

Before you were born your mother and I belonged to a colony. Flaking Scales and these old ones formed the matriarchy that ruled the colony. Then the Two-Headed One slaughtered the colony. We thought Flaking Scales was the only surviving matriarch. It turned out these five survived as well.

Brown Scale noticed that his mother and Yellow Claws were not with Flaking Scales and the Old Ones. He asked his father where they were. Male explained that the Old Ones had expelled White Sail and Yellow Claws from the matriarchy because the Old Ones considered them too young.

When did this happen? Brown Scale asked.

Last night, Male answered.

Do they have names?

The one with the red scales around the eyes is called Red Eyes. The one with the stooped shoulders used to be called Fish Finder. But taking off hurts her back and landing hurts her hips. So she no longer hunts for fish. Now she is called Stooped Shoulders. The one next to her still has strong bones, so she has held onto her youth name, Fish Finder.

They were both named Fish Finder?

Fish Finder is a common name and an important one. It designates who is the best at finding the largest groups of fish and the best tasting. Beside Fish Finder is Fertile Mother. She hatched eight broods. Each brood had no less than five eggs. I have been told she had laid up to nine eggs from one mating. This happened before your mother and I were born.

Do you believe that happened? Brown Scale sensed that his father doubted what he had been told.

No. Many Flock mates told me she was their mother. I could tell they were lying. They wanted the distinction of being born from a large brood. She probably did lay many eggs. How many, no one knows. I doubt Fertile Mother knows. She is so old. The last one is Crazy Crow. Her youth name was Fighter. Her matriarch never mated her because she was so good at protecting the broods of her Flock from predators. But old age scrambled her mind. So she is now called Crazy Crow.

What is a Crow?

You have never seen a crow. They are birds. Crazy birds.

The Old Ones were an unsettling sight. Stooped Shoulders and Crazy Crow had lost the manes that covered their spines, leaving the knobs of their vertebrae exposed. Red Eyes had no fur at all, while Fertile Mother's fur was long and mangy. Except for Fish Finder, the healthy "S" curve of their necks had sunken into a "U" curve and their shoulders stood up like two peaks, especially Stooped Shoulders'. Their colors were no longer bright and were marred by unwholesome shades of gray. The purple veins in their wings made it look as though they had worms trapped beneath the skin.

Male nudged Brown Scale to go and report what he had seen on his scouting mission to the matriarchs.

Brown Scale flew back to Razor Beak. She had her eyes shut in concentration.

Let's report our scouting mission, he said to her in thought.

She opened her eyes and said, *I made certain that I can only remember finding open sea. You should, too. These new matriarchs are very old. Their minds are powerful.*

Brown Scale closed his eyes and buried his memory of the island even deeper, covering them under detailed images of the water then clouded his mind further with the thoughts he and his father had shared with each other.

Red Eyes summoned them with a loud, grating caw.

Brown Scale and Razor Beak fluttered up to the matriarchs. The hill was crowded. Brown Scale and his sister had to stand before the giants halfway down the slope.

What did you find? Red Eyes demanded.

Brown Scale and Razor Beak showed them their memories of the open sea.

Is that all? Fish Finder asked. *I see a gap in your memories.*

It was a long flight, Razor Beak said. *We got bored. We must have forgotten what we saw.*

Did you get bored at the same time? Red Eyes narrowed her searing gaze.

Brown Scale and Razor Beak exchanged glances. Their throat pouches twitched nervously.

Yes, Brown Scale said.

Red Eyes turned to her fellow matriarchs to see if they believed the juveniles' story.

They frowned, unsure what to believe.

Probe their minds, Stooped Shoulders said.

Probe deep, Fish Finder added.

Flaking Scales and the Old Ones stared hard at Brown Scale and Razor Beak, peering deep into their minds. They tried to distract the aging pterosaurs with other memories, which only justified the matriarchs' suspicion. It got to a point where Brown Scale and Razor Beak could not help but recall the strange island that they had found and right at that moment Crazy Crow cawed victoriously.

Quiet, Red Eyes ordered her telepathically. *We can't concentrate.*

Crazy Crow started cackling and then cawed even louder.

Red Eyes stopped using telepathy and cawed at her to shut up.

Crazy Crow kept blathering incoherently.

The matriarchs stopped their probe.

Does it matter what they saw? Flaking Scales asked. *The juveniles can look for an island tomorrow.*

Red Eyes was reluctant to let Brown Scale and Razor Beak go. The others agreed with Flaking Scales. To the youngsters' relief they received permission to leave. They flew away from the hill, over the ridge, and down to the beach.

They saw our memories, Razor Beak said in thought, *but not clearly enough to see that we found an island.*

So long as they are not curious, our secret is safe, Brown Scale replied.

Were they curious?

That was a good question. Brown Scale was too nervous to gauge the matriarchs' mood.

So that is Brown Scale, Red Eyes said after he and his sister flew away. *You should not have let them go.*

If there is land out there, Flaking Scales said, *we will find it.*

Juveniles must never hide anything from their matriarchs. Red Eyes stewed in her juices.

110

The other matriarchs agreed that Flaking Scales had done a good job rebuilding the Flock, although they felt she should have killed White Sail's unnamed son, just in case he was weak. Weak blood contaminated the bloodline as much as deformed blood. On the other hand, they sympathized with her position. She was already unpopular for her efforts to kill Brown Scale. Meanwhile Brown Scale gained popularity. The problem was, as the Old Ones saw it, Flaking Scales was alone. Back in the days of the colony there were enough matriarchs to enforce unpopular, but necessary, decisions.

White Sail's male offspring might not be weak, Fish Finder said to salvage the situation. *He did not have a chance to fly home on his own.*

He can prove his worth in the next raid, Stooped Shoulders said.

So long as Brown Scale does not interfere, Red Eyes said. *He is a disruptive influence.*

He is, Flaking Scales conceded, *but don't try to kill him.*

We will kill him, Red Eyes assured her. *First we wait. Popularity is like a feather. One good puff of wind and it's gone. He will disappoint his Flock mates and when he does we can do whatever we like to him. His Flock mates will not care.*

Crazy Crow chittered excitedly as though she had a deep insight into their Brown Scale problem. The matriarch's gave her their attention. Once she had it, she started drooling.

At dawn the juveniles resumed their search for a new home. The matriarchs sent White Sail and Yellow Claws westward, in the same direction Brown Scale and Razor Beak had gone. They returned by nightfall, reporting that nothing was out there. Just open sea.

Red Eyes was convinced Brown Scale and Razor Beak had seen something. The other matriarchs were uneasy. How could two adults fail to find what two juveniles had found?

Locating a larger island took precedence, so the matter had to be dropped.

Brown Scale continued to mature at a rapid rate. After three weeks he had grown to forty meters in height. The matriarchs no longer seemed so godlike. He helped search for a new island so the Flock could establish their nesting ground there and he could go to the secret island that he had found and live by himself.

No suitable island had been found, but a school of waterborne fighting machines had been spotted toward the northeast. The matriarchs assembled the juveniles around the hill. They had grown too much to stand on the slope.

Red Eyes spoke to them through telepathy.

The Gray Sister found fresh prey for your next raid. Show them what you found, Gray Sister.

The unmated Gray Sister showed the juveniles her memory of the human machines. One was as massive as a small island. Eight little machines sailed alongside its flanks. What was exciting about the big machine was that it carried a swarm of flying machines.

This is your chance to prove to the humans that we are the masters of the sky, Red Eyes told them. *Their flying machines are faster than you, but you are more agile. Use your agility to your advantage.*

Slaughter them! White Sail cawed.

Slaughter them all! Yellow Claws added. *The sky is ours! Not the apes'!*

The juveniles cawed, chanting, *Slaughter them! Slaughter them!*

Wait on the ridge, Flaking Scales told the juveniles. *When your mothers are ready they will lead you.*

The juveniles flapped over to the ridge, whipping up clouds of dust in their wake.

Brown Scale, wait, Red Eyes called to him.

Brown Scale paused at the bottom of the hill.

Red Eyes turned to Flaking Scales. Flaking Scales spoke.

Do not help the injured. Let them fly home on their own.

What if they can't? Brown Scale asked.

Leave them, Red Eyes said, butting in on Flaking Scales. *The raids cull the Flock of its weak members.*

Brown Scale frowned at her.

Did you notice how weak and fragile the humans are? Fertile Mother asked.

They are tasty, too, Brown Scale rejoined.

Fertile Mother cackled. *Yes, they are. They became weak because they protected the weaker members of their kind. That is why they build machines, to make themselves strong again. We don't want to become like them. Do you understand?*

Forsaking the injured seemed cruel and impractical. The more members the Flock had the stronger their mental faculties became. That's what gave them the edge over the predators. However, the fate of the Flock wasn't going to be Brown Scale's concern once he became an adult. So he complied with the matriarchs' wishes.

Seeing that he was compliant, they dismissed him from their hill.

He flew to his father, who was watching the eggs. The Gray Sister he had chosen as his mate had flown off. It was her turn to get food.

Brown Scale asked Male if he had fought flying machines.

Yes. Fighting them is fun.

Show me your memories. I want to see how they fight.

Male recalled his memories. Brown Scale read his mind and saw that the flying machines had a pebble shooter inside of their heads. They also fired slender logs from under their wings. The logs were smooth with a pointed tip on one end and spat fire from the other. The logs could follow its prey wherever it went.

Watch out for the fire logs, his father warned. *They can knock you senseless if they hit you in the head. The pebble shooter won't hurt you much unless the machine can get close. Then the pebbles can shred your wings. Once you get as big as I am, these machines won't be able to harm you.*

I am almost as big as you now, Brown Scale pointed out.

You certainly are! His father proudly scratched the top of his beak. *Your mother will leave soon. Join your siblings.*

Brown Scale flapped over to his siblings on the ridge. They were gathered around the pebble shooter Brown Scale had brought home from their last raid. It reminded them of their superiority over the humans.

While they waited, Brown Scale reviewed his father's memories and noticed that the fire logs were no more maneuverable than the flying machines. He clucked to his siblings, asking them to gather around. They formed a circle and pressed their heads together so Brown Scale could show them his battle plan. Then he called Yellow Claws' offspring together and showed them.

Brown Scale's unnamed brother was under a lot of pressure to prove his worth.

The matriarchs told me I mustn't help you, Brown Scale said to him.

Don't! His brother replied indignantly.

Follow the plan and none of us will be injured.

I must risk getting injured. I have to show the matriarchs that I am strong. They might kill me if they see that I am weak.

You will look stupid if you are the only one who comes home hurt.

Anger flashed in his brother's eyes.

White Sail and Yellow Claws fetched their broods and along with the unmated Gray Sister flew northeast to engage the humans.

Brown Scale felt a tingling sensation. White Sail clucked at the Gray Sister. The gray Flock pterosaur broke from their formation and headed further east and chased a flying machine out of the clouds. The odd-looking contraption had a large disk on its back. It tried to escape but was too slow. The Gray Sister rammed into the disk with her keel, sending the machine careening out of the air. The tingling sensation ceased.

Ten more machines burst from the clouds. They were smaller, sleeker, closing fast. White Sail and Yellow Claws withdrew to give the juveniles room to fight. Brown Scale cawed at his peers to initiate his attack plan. They flew like a cloud of flies, crossing each other's paths in random circles. The humans launched their fire logs. The logs left a trail of smoke as they hissed toward Brown Scale's formation and chased after the young pterosaurs. Razor Beak flew passed Peeps with a log on her tail. Before the log could score a hit, Peeps snapped it in half with her beak. A log was also chasing her, but Brown Scale was already circling around toward Peeps and managed to grab it before it could hit her.

Brown Scale's unnamed brother grabbed a log that was trailing one of Yellow Claws' offspring. He spat out the crushed weapon and clucked, *got one!*

Then one of Yellow Claws' female offspring clucked, *got one!*

Another clucked twice, *I got two!*

The humans' attempt to kill them turned into a game. Before long the juveniles ran out of fire logs to catch.

Undeterred, the humans kept coming.

With a caw Brown Scale signaled the two broods to attack. He led the charge. Both groups were coming at each other so quickly the distance between them vanished within moments. The humans barely fired a few rounds from their pebble shooters when Brown Scale's team banked out of the way and attacked the machines as they passed, ramming them with their keels. The machines shattered like eggs. Pieces hurled in every direction. Most of the humans managed to pop out of their flyers and release a wing membrane. The sight of them dangling from these membranes sent the juveniles into a feeding frenzy.

Two machines escaped unmolested.

Brown Scale and his Flock mates pursued.

Gradually, the two flying machines slipped ahead of them. The waterborne machines were out on the horizon. They were no longer heading southwest, but had turned around and were heading northeast. More flyers were taking off from the deck of the giant machine. As they drew near, Brown Scale had his Flock mates reduce speed so they could execute his battle plan again.

Peeps squawked in excitement and dove for the giant machine.

Brown Scale called her back but she was too far ahead to hear him. He had expected his brother to be

I Shall Not Mate

reckless, not her. Clucking to his Flock mates, he ordered them to attack the flyers and remember what the matriarchs had said. Use your agility to your advantage.

As the young pterosaurs brawled with the flying machines up in the clouds, Brown Scale dove after Peeps.

The weapons aboard the waterborne machines coughed, puffed, and chattered. Peeps pierced the firestorm and soared over the deck of the big ship. The winds kicked up by her wake blew over the humans and flipped their flying machines on top of each other. Explosions erupted. The deck was in disarray.

Brown Scale drew some of the fire off of her, but not enough. Three logs tracked Peeps. She banked sharply to the left, right, up and down, then around in a tight circle, shaking two logs. The third struck her hip. She screeched and fell into the water. In the next instant a log smashed into Brown Scale's chest. Fire and splinters raked his body. The blow knocked him out of the air. He crashed into one of the smaller waterborne machines. It rolled in one direction and then rolled back in the other. He clung to the superstructure as it capsized. Sea water rushed into his nostrils and down his throat. Salt stung his eyes. Swirling bubbles blurred his vision. There was no telling which way led to the surface. He scrambled up the side of the craft, breaking to the sun-kissed air.

Coughing up water, he slumped onto the belly of the steel beast. When he regained his strength, he searched for Peeps.

She was flailing in the sea, unable to get back into the air. Her blood was turning the water around her red. The human weapon had torn her wing membrane from her leg. With a torn wing, she was not likely to escape. Exhausted, she laid flat like a leaf. If she was

117

lucky she would float like one, but she was not going to be lucky. Water seeped through the holes in her wings caused by the pebble shooters. She let out a plaintive, gurgling peep.

The matriarchs had forbidden him to help his Flock mates.

Perhaps he could make it easier for her to help herself.

He took off and grabbed the stern of the capsized watercraft in his beak and pushed it toward her. Its great weight resisted his efforts. Flapping hard, the machine budged bit by bit and slid slowly toward Peeps.

The nearby machines harangued him. The report of their guns popped in his ears as their ordnance punched his body.

Razor Beak soared overhead, squawking at the machines to get them to shoot at her instead. The other juveniles dropped atop the machines, pecking them with their beaks. The machines coordinated their fire against the juveniles. Their wings would be shredded long before they could kill the machines.

Brown Scale squawked for attention and then broadcasted his memory of how he had capsized his machine. The juveniles understood. Capsize the machines and the humans could no longer fire their weapons.

They took off and flew high above the battle area. Diving back down at top speed, they tackled the machines' superstructures. The machines capsized. By the time the last drops of water splashed back into the sea, the guns fell silent.

Brown Scale pushed his machine within reach. Peeps clawed her way up atop its belly and lay there in the sun, panting.

Brown Scale perched on the other end.

The other juveniles perched on their capsized machines.

The big watercraft continued sailing.

The juveniles pleaded for their mothers to come topple the big machine before it got away.

As a rule, the mothers did not participate in a raid. But the raid was ostensibly over, so they flew down from the clouds and pounced upon the large craft. An alarm squealed. Yellow Claws and White Sail hung onto the side of the craft. It listed to the side. Wreckage slid off the deck and splashed into the water. Yet, the stubborn vessel refused to flip. The Gray Sister added her weight, finally forcing the craft on end. Its deck stood perpendicular to the sea. The three adults flapped to the top edge and shifted their weight to force the metal behemoth to tip onto its back. The flat deck hit the waves with a loud crash.

The juveniles cheered and flapped their wings.

The three adults stood atop their kill. Once they caught their breath they led the two broods home. Peeps lagged far behind. Brown Scale lagged midway between the Flock and his sister so a predator would not see her as an easy kill.

His mother flew up beside Brown Scale and glared at him. Helping his sister would convince the matriarchs that she was weak.

I'm tired, he chittered. *It's hard to keep up.*

White Sail thought about what he really meant. Lowering the sail atop her head she glanced back at her struggling daughter.

I'm tired, too, White Sail chittered.

Together they lagged behind to protect Peeps.

Brown Scale's unnamed brother racked up the highest kill score from the raid. He grabbed thirty-nine fire logs, wrecked eleven flyers, ate nine humans, and capsized one waterborne machine. In return he sustained superficial injuries. Within a day or so there would not be a mark on him. The matriarchs declared him fit and useful for future breeding. He strut about the island on all fours with his head up, proud that he had shed the stigma of being weak.

The matriarchs were none the wiser of the help Brown Scale and his mother had afforded Peeps. She was able to heal without fear of being culled. As for her kill score, no one was sure how much damage she had caused on the deck of the big ship. Only the kills she had made in the air were counted. Peeps didn't dispute the final tally because Brown Scale and her mother had helped her survive. Since someone helped her, she helped her unnamed brother secure his survival by being silent so he could gain recognition.

After a few days White Sail's offspring reached adulthood. In human terms only several months had elapsed from the time that they had hatched to the time that they grew up. To the offspring it seemed like a long, hard journey.

For Brown Scale the journey had been perilous. It was a heady moment. His instincts told him he had mastered the things he needed to survive on his own. He could fight. He could fly long distances. He could feed himself and find fresh water. And most importantly, he had a place to go—the fog-enshrouded island.

Brown Scale lingered with the Flock a while longer. It was wise not to be too hasty.

Yellow Claws' offspring reached breeding age. Excitement stirred the Flock. There were two breeding age males available for this mating season. Male was still preoccupied with the Gray Sister's brood.

Red Eyes called Brown Scale's unnamed brother and Yellow Claws' one son, Hooked Claw, to the hill.

White Sail beckoned Brown Scale to follow her to the hill.

Out of curiosity he followed her.

White Sail told the matriarchs through telepathy that this season they had three breeding age males. Not two.

The matriarchs gave her dirty looks.

Brown Scale is deformed! Flaking Scales reminded her.

Brown Scale is my son, White Sail replied.

Her statement shocked Brown Scale. Memories of her trying to kill him when he was a newborn replayed in his mind.

White Sail sensed them and turned to him with regret in her good eye.

You were ashamed of him, Flaking Scales returned.

I was wrong, White Sail said.

He scarred your eye! You are half blind.

Because you told me to kill him. By blinding me, he proved he was fit to survive. He even made you cower. White Sail revealed her memory of Flaking Scales shirking way from a tiny, fluttering newborn.

Embarrassed, Flaking Scales retracted her head between her shoulders.

Her fellow matriarchs glowered at her.

He shall not mate! Red Eyes shouted with her thoughts. *He shall not mate,* she repeated to the whole Flock. *Obey the matriarchy.*

Brown Scale left the gathered pterosaurs and headed for his roosting place. He was too overcome with emotion to fly, emotions which were rarely felt by a flying reptile. There was a mixture of melancholy and vindication, even some joy.

His mother cawed at him to come back.

He kept going.

Sitting in his roost by the sea, he wondered as he watched the tide beat against the rocks if he still had a reason to leave.

Razor Beak landed on the rocky shore, outside his nook. She knew what was weighing on him. The hive mind of the Flock allowed her to see clearly.

Stay, she chirped.

Brown Scale tried to avoid eye contact, but couldn't. Razor Beak cared about him before their other siblings were fully cognizant that he was their brother.

I sense that I belong to the Flock, he confessed. *I also sense that my place is to be on my own.*

You are learning how to belong, she said. *You will master belonging like you have mastered everything else, Hatchling Leader.*

He cackled.

Razor Beak cackled, too.

The nickname sounded childish now that they were grown up.

Brown Scale climbed out of his nook. *The island is waiting for me. That is where I belong.*

The island is a terrible place. Don't go.

The island welcomed me. You did not notice because your mind weakened when we left the Flock. That is a secret I kept from you. My mind does not weaken when I am alone. Everyone else's does. You need to stay together. I don't need to stay with anyone. I was born to be alone.

If we find a new home, how will you find us? Razor Beak asked.

Brown Scale was unsure. He was also unsure of what to say to his sister. Flock pterosaurs never learned the concept of goodbye.

He looked at her one more time, a long time so he would have a solid memory of her to take with him, and to leave her with a solid memory of him.

Then he took off for the fog-enshrouded island.

14

After Tylogon had been driven off, the *Haruo-maru* rolled upside right. Miraculously, none of her crew had been killed, but most sustained concussions and broken bones. The ship had also taken on a lot of water. Captain Takagi ordered the *Haruo* to return to its home port. The research vessel accompanied the craft.

Down two vessels, Takagi's task force continued due south. Inoue's group was two days away. The two captains agreed to link up and proceed to the location where Shindo believed to be the brown Flock pterosaur's home island.

Despite the loss of the two vessels, Shindo and his companions felt optimistic.

Then bad news hit.

A US Navy aircraft carrier out on maneuvers had been attacked by the Flock. The armored juvenile had been sighted among the flying kaiju. The beast was estimated to be thirty to forty meters in height with a hundred meter wingspan. Shindo's quarry was getting close to reaching adulthood. It flipped one of the carrier's escorts. After it did so, its fellow reptiles copied its actions, capsizing the entire battlegroup, including the aircraft carrier. The carrier was a *Nimitz*-class ship—a one hundred thousand ton ship—the largest military craft sailing the sea was spun like a river log.

The Japanese government granted her US ally's request for assistance since Japan had ships within the area. Those ships were Inoue's. Not only was the Flock becoming more dangerous, Takagi lost three more combat ships to a rescue mission.

Captain Takagi reminded Shindo that he might be able to get the mission aborted since the prime minister wasn't keen on it to begin with.

Shindo refused. There was still hope.

About a week's left of hope, according to Professor Abe's estimation of the creature's growth rate.

Each day that passed without any sign of the island or a Flock kaiju brought the sun down lower on that hope.

"Do you ever have any doubts about what you're doing?" Yomo asked Shindo. They were in Shindo's cabin.

"Of course," Shindo said.

"How about now?"

"Especially now."

Yomo frowned in all seriousness. "Then why go on?"

"Because doubt is often based on fear. Not reason."

"Often. But not always. Doubt can be your reason trying to speak to you."

"Not this time."

"How can you be sure?"

"Because," Shindo said, "I'm scared we will end up like the American's carrier. How about you, Yomo? Are you scared?"

"Of course! I feel helpless. Wherever this boat goes you go and if it sinks you go down with it. I'm used to being on land where you always have the option to run."

Over the intercom Captain Takagi told Shindo to come up to the bridge. Fast.

As he and Yomo ran to see the captain the ship went on combat alert. Three unidentified flying objects had been spotted on radar. They flew on the outer edges of the radar's range. One object circled in the air and dropped in altitude, down to the sea and then followed after the other two objects. It behaved just like an animal dropping down to grab a fish. The objects proceeded in an easterly direction and then flew south east, out of range.

"What do you think?" the captain asked Shindo.

"It's the Flock. Expect an attack."

The day passed. No attack came.

No attack came the following day.

Shindo spent his time on the bridge with a pair of binoculars, scanning the horizon for land.

"Something else must be shaking," Shindo said. "The Flock should have come after us by now."

"What do you think is happening?" Sayoko asked. She had the fire controls to the laser cannon online and ready to fire.

"Mating season."

"Then we're too late," Captain Takagi concluded.

"Not quite." Shindo scanned the horizon again. "It takes several weeks for Flock eggs to hatch. So, after we kill the brown kaiju we send a helicopter over the island, locate their nesting sites, and destroy every egg we can find."

"We haven't found the island yet," the captain said.

"It's out there. Keep going south."

A new clue arrived on the brown Flock pterosaur's location. Shindo received an electronic dispatch in his portable computer's inbox from his chief, Goro Yamashita. The dispatch included satellite photos. The nature of the photos required Captain Takagi and Sayoko to sign a nondisclosure agreement. The photos were that sensitive.

They gathered in the captain's quarters.

Once Shindo obtained their signatures, he opened his laptop and put the most important photo in the collection on the screen.

"Our satellite hit the jackpot yesterday," he said. "Here it is."

The photo was of the brown Flock pterosaur. It was adult size and in good health. The wings were outstretched. Even from orbit, the animal looked magnificent. The armored plating on its neck, shoulders and back were clearly visible in the shot along with the conical spikes running down the middle of its back.

But that pterosaur was not the reason why the photo was classified.

A quarter of it could not be seen, specifically the head and part of the right wing. It was as if it were photographed while in the process of disappearing into thin air.

Shindo put up the next photo. The flying reptile had moved further across the satellite's view. Half of the creature could not be seen.

In the next photo only its feet were visible.

In the last photo, it was gone. All the satellite captured was open water.

"Does the monster have the ability to make itself invisible?" Sayoko asked.

"No," Shindo answered. "This location photographed by the satellite is seven hundred nautical miles due east of New Zealand. The intelligence agencies of five countries have a file describing what's here. In those five agencies only a handful of living persons are aware these files exist."

"And you're one of the few," Sayoko said.

Shindo nodded. "Captain Takagi, being a seaman, I imagine you know more about this subject than I do. Why don't you tell them?"

The captain smiled. He was glad to.

Sayoko and Yomo gave Takagi their undivided attention.

"The photos only show water. But there is an island there. It doesn't want to be seen. That's why the brown Flock pterosaur appears to be vanishing. As it passes over the land, it too becomes invisible."

"An invisible island?" Sayoko asked, sounding skeptical.

"It can be seen when it wants to be seen and it has been seen by Man four times. The government dismissed most of the legends tied to this island because they are too fantastic to believe. Those of us who sail these waters, we cannot afford to forget them, so we pass them on by word of mouth.

"The island was first discovered around 1000 AD. A Polynesian man and his four friends sailed there in their long boat canoe. Two of the man's friends watched their boat while he and his other two companions explored the interior. It was hot and humid. The plants were strange and barren of fruit. One of the man's companions died from a spider bite. The other lost his foot to a fat salamander that was as big as a crocodile. His friend bled to death. The man ran back to the boat only to have his path blocked by a boulder. Lounging atop the boulder was a giant lizard with a sail on its back like a fish. The lizard spoke to him without moving its mouth. It told him this land was sacred. The man pleaded for his life. The lizard said he may live so long as he promised to tell his people to stay off the island. The man promised. The lizard and boulder vanished. The man kept his promise. The story spread to the settlements across the South Pacific.

"But three centuries later people no longer took the story seriously, except for the fact that there was an uninhabited island waiting to be colonized. The Maoris sent out an expedition. They found the island and nearly every member of the expedition died right where they landed on the shore. The survivors said a yellow fog seeped out of the sand like sweat from a man's pours. It stunk like rotten eggs and burned the inside of their chest. If this story can be taken at face value, I'd say they were attacked by sulfuric gas."

"So the island is volcanic," Yomo concluded.

The captain gave him a cryptic grin and motioned to him to wait. There was more. "In 1592, a storm blew two Spanish galleons off course. They spotted the island and sailed toward it to restock their provisions. As the lead vessel neared a grotto, the sea began to boil. Molten rock rose up underneath it and crushed the ship like a giant hand. The timbers snapped like tried sticks in its grip. The sailors on the other ship could hear the screams of the crew. The molten hand pulled the galleon underwater. Wreckage floated on the turbulent waters where the ship was a moment ago. The captain of the second ship ordered his men to turn their vessel around. They didn't need to. A massive wave swept them away from the island. By the time the wave released the ship, the captain and his men could only see the black peaks of the island's mountains in the distance.

"The Spanish took the hint and avoided that region since.

"Captain James Cook became the next man to find the island. The British Royal Society had commissioned him to verify if a southern continent called Terra Australis existed in the South Pacific. In 1773, in the early hours of the morning, the island had been spotted off the portside. Cook suspected he had found the land so many explorers had described. He took a dozen armed sailors ashore with him. He felt a peculiarly strong notion that if his men explored the interior with him they would die whereas he would be safe.

"His men waited at the boat while he trudged through a mountain pass, alone, into a mist covered valley. He drew illustrations into his journal of the creatures and plants he discovered. As he followed a stream he found a giant sail-backed reptile lounging on a boulder. It seemed to have been waiting for him. Cook said the lizard spoke with him for hours about the island's flora and fauna. Then the lizard asked the British captain if he liked his home.

"Captain Cook asked his host to be specific. Did it mean his house in England or his country in general?

"'Whichever you consider your home,' the lizard said.

"'All right,' the captain said, 'I consider my country my home.'

"'Would you appreciate it if someone replaced your neighbors with other people, uprooted your trees and planted new ones, and erased your landscape?'

"Cook thought the question was odd. He humored the lizard and said, 'No, I wouldn't appreciate it.'

"'Neither would I,' the lizard said." Captain Takagi snapped his fingers. "In the next instant Captain Cook found himself aboard his ship. He felt uneasy, to the point where he thought he was going to become ill. He called his men who were still waiting for him on the shore back to the ship and set sail. When he returned home he told no one. But his men talked about the island. Word reached the Royal Society. Cook had no choice but to surrender his journal and give an account of what happened.

"The Royal Society was beside themselves. James Cook was their star explorer. Yet, as learned men the Society could not accept his story.

"Cook promised to never speak of the island unless authorized by the Society.

"Satisfied, the Royal Society dropped the matter, although they could not deny an island had been found and decided that this must be the southern continent previous explorers had spoken about. The Society recognized the island as Terra Australis. That is until the following century when paleontologists found fossils of animals and plants which were identical to the illustrations in Cook's journal. All of them were consistent with the ecosystem that existed during the Permian Period. Then in the twentieth century, Alfred Wegener figured out that the Earth's continents had formed one supercontinent. He called it Pangea. Either of you want to guess when this continent formed?"

Sayoko tackled the question. "During the Permian Period."

"Correct. At the start of the Permian to be exact. The Royal Society believed the island must be a remnant of that continent. They changed its name to Pangea Island.

"The British government confiscated all materials relating to Cook's exploration of the island and swore the Society to secrecy.

"Then during the Pacific War one of our submarines discovered Pangea Island while on reconnaissance. The captain did not see any sign of the Allies through his periscope. He surfaced and sent a party ashore to survey the island. Sub-lieutenant

Tetsutaro Ito was in charge of the landing party. Like Captain Cook, Ito felt that he was the only one who could safely explore the interior. He left a guard at the boat and split the rest of his men into two parties and had them walk along the coast to get the breadth of the island, but under no circumstances were they to leave the shore. Ito then trekked through a mountain pass and found the mist-filled valley. He saw the same animals and plants that Cook had seen. He also found the stream which led to the boulder where the giant sail-backed lizard rested. The lizard greeted him by name and asked, without moving its mouth, if it was true that it was his duty to die for the Emperor.

"Ito said it was.

"'Then you came to the right place,' the lizard said. 'This island is where men come to die.'

"Taken aback, Ito said, 'The Emperor does not want his soldiers to die in vain.'

"'You should tell him', the lizard said, 'so he does not build a base here.'

"In the next moment Ito woke up in bed, at home, in Sasebo. He thought he must have dreamt the whole incident. But he was still in his uniform. His mother was shocked to find him in his room. He turned himself in at the naval base in Sasebo and explained what happened with the caveat that he did not expect to be believed. The officer he spoke to didn't accept his story. Ito begged the officer to have a message radioed to his captain, warning him to call the landing party back to the sub before any of them stepped inland.

"The navy was in a tight spot. If they didn't accept his story, then Ito could be accused of desertion. Then he would have to stand trial. His story would go on the record. There was no way anyone could explain how he returned home while his ship was still at sea. They would have to admit, for the public record, that he had been teleported by an unknown force. The navy discharged Ito instead, swore him to secrecy, and sent him to work in a Mitsubishi factory building fighters for the duration of the war.

"After the war, Ito researched prehistoric animals at the library to identify what he had seen on the island. He found out that the sail-backed lizard he had spoken to wasn't a lizard. It was a pelycosaur called a *Dimetrodon*."

Takagi paused again.

"But something wasn't right," he continued. "The books said a *Dimetrodon* was four meters long. The beast Ito saw was five times that length. And of course the books didn't say anything about the dimetrodons having telepathy.

"Captain Cook wrote in his journal that the creature identified itself as the island's spokesman. Ito told my mother the same thing, except he believed the *Dimetrodon* was misleading him. He believed the giant *Dimetrodon* was the flesh and blood manifestation of the island itself."

"How did your mother meet Ito?" Sayoko asked.

Captain Takagi swiveled in his chair so they could see a small black and white photo of a young man in an Imperial Navy uniform. The photo was in a gold frame, mounted to the wall. "Tetsutaro Ito is my great grandfather."

Sayoko caught her breath.

Takagi swiveled back to face them. "After the war, the US occupation forces uncovered my great grandfather's account in the Imperial Navy records. They sent aircraft over the area. They found nothing. No search succeeded since. My great grandfather was the last person to have set foot on the island."

"Pangea Island can't hide anymore," Shindo said. "The satellite data gives us the exact longitude and latitude coordinates of where these photos were taken."

"It sounds like to me," Yomo said, "Pangea Island wants to remain as is with its Permian ecosystem. So why was our brown Flock pterosaur allowed to go there? It's a modern day animal. Not a Permian one."

"The brown pterosaur is not going to build a port, hotels, and resorts," Sayoko said. "That's what we would do if we settled there."

"I'd advise not going to the island," Captain Takagi said. "The government has kept that place secret to keep curiosity seekers out of there. Who knows what you're going to stir up?"

"Think about it, Shindo," Yomo said in earnest. "What if the entire Flock is living there? We will be taking on the Flock and the island."

Shindo thought up a new plan. "We can wait five kilometers off Pangea's coast. That should be far enough away to satisfy it. If we're lucky the Flock will come to us."

"What about the eggs?" Yomo asked. "We'll have to go to the island to make sure there are no nests."

Shindo tried a different tact. "All right." He threw his hands up. "Let's radio the Chief and tell him the mission is hopeless. But what are we going to do if the armored pterosaur's traits spread to the next generation, and the next, and the next after that?"

He looked to his partner Yomo.

Yomo didn't have an answer.

He looked to Sayoko.

She didn't have an answer.

He looked to Captain Takagi.

Captain Takagi turned back to the photo of his great grandfather, sighed, and said, "I guess we change course for Pangea Island."

15

After Tiamatodon destroyed the Flock colony, he returned to Bajo Island, his birthplace. Bajo was famous for its Jurassic fauna. The name itself was derived from the Bajocian stage of the Jurassic period. It was given that name because the animals on that island were identical to the animals found fossilized in Bajocian-age rock.

Tiamatodon left deep prints on the beach as he strode inland, crushing trees underfoot.

The birds warned the other animals with shrill warbling, calling out *Giant predator! Giant predator!*

Tiamatodon scattered a herd of cetiosaurs as he marched into a clearing. The cetiosaurs were modest-sized sauropods—five meters high and fourteen meters long. They were like ferrets in comparison to Tiamatodon. Tiamatodon's long strides overtook them. Several were crushed and then steamrolled by his tail. He left a trail of broken bodies. The survivors stampeded into the jungle. The jungle canopy hid them from view but their bleats could be heard.

Tiamatodon ignored them. His eyes were set on the ocean on the far side of the island. Even though Bajo was his home, it was nothing more than an obstacle to be crossed.

The two-headed beast stopped when he spotted the bunker. Wind, rain, and years had chipped away at its hard walls, yet it still stood. This was where Tiamatodon had been hatched. The humans had never returned to this facility ever since he broke out of his pen. Tiamatodon was actually two creatures, a male and a female. A Siamese twin. The male half was indifferent toward the bunker. For the female the bunker triggered memories of their past. They didn't fully understand how they came to be but they were able to read the minds of the humans who incubated their egg. The humans had subjected them to a form of energy that fused them together. Their instincts told them that the energy had turned them into something unnatural.

A female megalosaur stepped out of the bunker's exit that lead to the pens where the other test subjects had been kept. She hissed at Tiamatodon, warning the Siamese twin to back away. Her mate hopped atop the bunker. His one-ton weight made a hearty thump when he landed atop the structure. He uttered a one-note call which drew a little over forty megalosaurs out of the jungle. They surrounded Tiamatodon like crows around a falcon. They roared and rooted the ground with their feet, threatening to attack en masse.

Tiamatodon figured the female must be a mother and her nest was inside the abandoned building.

The megalosaurs did not recognize Tiamatodon as one of their own even though the twin-headed monster was of their kind. That was the extent of the kaiju's mutation. The beast was no longer of the same color. Instead of being a brownish olive with yellow striping, Tiamatodon was all black. He and his sister did not have the scent of a *Megalosaurus*. They had no arms and they stood upright like a human.

Tiamatodon, on the other hand, did recognize their kinship with the megalosaurs, and yet felt no solidarity. The twin-headed beast roared back, drowning out the roars of the megalosaurs. The echo rocked the jungle.

The megalosaurs stood their ground. If they ran, the animals they preyed upon would lose their fear of them. Their prey would fight rather than run, making it harder to get enough to eat. The mother guarding the bunker exit snapped at Tiamatodon's ankle. The others followed suit. They were hopelessly outmatched in size, but numbers could intimidate large animals. No one liked pain, not even the giants.

Tiamatodon knew this was just a scare tactic. He and his sister followed up their roars with a blast of their plasma rays. The female half of Tiamatodon spewed her rays at the megalosaurs on the left. The rays bowled over the theropod dinosaurs. Their bodies were burnt to a crisp before they stopped rolling. The male half torched the megalosaurs on the right. The smell of burnt meat filled the air. The sweep of the plasma rays lit the undergrowth. The flames spread to the treetops. Tiamatodon then stomped on the mother, crushing her under his tremendous weight. Tiamatodon then strode forward, leaving the father megalosaur alone atop the bunker. Tiamatodon did not spare the father out of mercy. He and his sister did so out of cruelty. The father was now on his own with a nest to guard and no mate or pack for support.

While Brown Scale was growing up, Tiamatodon was swimming due south. By the time Brown Scale and Razor Beak had discovered Pangea Island, Tiamatodon had crossed the equator. The twin-headed beast was also heading for Pangea.

Tiamatodon had tried and failed to locate the island. The Siamese twin had sensed the presence of the island's spirit. So Tiamatodon knew the island's whereabouts, but whenever Tiamatodon drew near, the spirit scrambled the monster's senses, preventing the Two-Headed One from making landfall. Tiamatodon wanted to reach the island because it could also sense the presence of the animals. That was what Tiamatodon wanted. To kill the animals.

Several weeks later, after Brown Scale had made Pangea Island his home, Tiamatodon drew near once again. Tiamatodon was still too far away for him to see the island, but he could sense the presence of the island's spirit.

Tiamatodon slowed to a halt in the water and concentrated on the spirit's presence. When both the male and female halves memorized where the spirit was, Tiamatodon swam toward it. He kept both heads above water. He was certain enough of the distance that he had a good idea of how soon he should see land on the horizon. He and his sister stayed focus on their course. So long as they did not waver they should be able to reach the shore no matter how much the spirit scrambled their perception.

An hour passed.

Then another.

Tiamatodon was as sluggish in the water as he was on land. It would take time to reach his destination.

The third hour passed.

By now land should be cropping up into view. Tiamatodon became impatient. He could sense with his psychic ability that the spirit was closer than before. Land should be visible. Tiamatodon swam faster. If necessary he would beach himself. The spirit may be able to make its island invisible but there was no way it could make the land intangible.

The fourth hour past. Tiamatodon sensed that the island spirit was behind him. That would be impossible. He would have seen land as he passed the spirit. The spirit was tied to the land. Wherever the island spirit was, there was island.

Tiamatodon halted in the water. The male half searched the horizon all around. The female half told him to keep going. *Don't look around,* she told her brother in thought, *or we will lose sight of the direction we have been going.*

Tiamatodon resumed course. The island spirit seemed to be falling further behind them. It had to be a psychic trick. Yet both halves of the two-headed beast had doubts. Tiamatodon swam to the ocean bottom to see if the ocean floor had been becoming shallower or deeper. In either case there should be a slope leading toward dry land.

The ocean bottom was flat.

In case the island spirit was tricking Tiamatodon's two sets of eyes he planted both feet on the ground.

The ocean floor felt flat.

Tiamatodon swam back up for air. Despite the monster's heightened intelligence and psychic ability, the Two-Headed One was an animal. It was difficult for animals to distrust their five senses. When Tiamatodon's senses told him the ocean floor was flat and there was no island in sight, then he felt he had to conclude he had missed the island. Yet his instinct told him his senses were being lied to.

But if that was a fact then what was the truth? Where was he? Where was the island?

Then Tiamatodon sensed five ships approaching from the northeast. Judging by the number of humans in each vessel, the group included a destroyer, three frigates, and an unarmed craft. The destroyer was armed with a laser cannon. Tiamatodon could sense the confidence humans felt when they had a beam weapon at their disposal.

The twin-headed beast gulped a lung-full of air and then dived deep into the ocean before the ships sailed close enough to detect it on sonar. At the cold, deep bottom, Tiamatodon waited. After several hours the ships passed overhead. After another hour they were far enough away for Tiamatodon to surface.

As they passed overhead, Tiamatodon had read their minds and learned that they were searching for Pangea Island, too. The island spirit could fool the senses of a living being. It might not be able to fool the humans' machines.

Tiamatodon decided to follow the ships.

Part 3

16

White Sail and Yellow Claws' females built shallow nests and made half-hearted attempts to attract the males. The females desired Brown Scale instead. They wanted cunning offspring with armored plates. They did not want any Pearly Whites in their broods, which would likely happen if they mated with Brown Scale's unnamed brother and Yellow Claws' male offspring, Hooked Claw.

The unnamed brother and Hooked Claw felt put out. They were healthy. They had proved themselves in battle. It was their right to breed, or at least be given the respect they had earned. They resented Brown Scale. He made them feel obsolete.

The females became resentful, too. They felt Brown Scale had abandoned them.

Red Eyes gained renown among the matriarchs because her prediction came true. Popularity was fleeting. Now the matriarchs could kill Brown Scale.

They waited until Razor Beak was alone, on the beach, out of sight from the rest of the Flock, when they swooped down on her, surrounding her on the black sand.

Razor Beak recoiled out of reflex and hissed.

Unfazed, Red Eyes stared down at the young female. The Flock hive mind made it clear to Razor Beak that the matriarchs intended to kill her brother. First, they needed to know where he went. Red Eyes ordered her to tell them.

Razor Beak feigned ignorance.

That didn't get her anywhere. Everyone knew Razor Beak and Brown Scale were close.

The matriarchs waited for their answer.

Before her thoughts could betray Brown Scale, Razor Beak took off.

She failed to notice that Crazy Crow was not with the matriarchs. No sooner had she got off the ground, Crazy Crow pounced on her from above, slamming her belly- first into the moist sand. Red Eyes stomped on Razor Beak's wing finger. A crack snapped from the finger's joint.

Razor Beak screeched.

Crazy Crow gurgled, dripping drool onto Razor Beak's white fur.

Red Eyes circled back around and stared hard into Razor Beak's eyes. With her telepathy she spoke one word: *Where?*

Razor Beak used her lack of understanding of Pangea Island as a lack of knowledge for its location and said, *I don't know!*

The matriarchs saw through her deception.

Red Eyes clucked to Fish Finder, the strongest of the matriarchs.

Fish Finder stepped on Razor Beak's dislocated finger.

Red Eyes repeated her question.

Razor Beak closed her eyes, concentrated, blanking her mind.

Red Eyes flicked her gaze to the other matriarchs, rallying them to do what needed to be done.

As one they probed Razor Beak's mind, forced the memories of her last contact with Brown Scale out of the dark recesses. They saw the brown deformity climb out of his nook on the coast. Heard his thoughts: *The island is waiting for me. That is where I belong.* They heard her thoughts: *The island is a terrible place. Don't go.* They heard his response: *The island welcomed me. You did not notice because your mind weakened when we left the Flock. That is a secret I kept from you. My mind does not weaken when I am alone. Everyone else's does. You need to stay together. I don't need to stay with anyone. I was born to be alone.*

Then they saw him take flight, heading due west.

Just as the matriarchs thought. Brown Scale and Razor Beak did find an island. Red Eyes ordered Razor Beak to show them where it was.

Razor Beak refused to dredge up anymore incriminating memories. She snapped at Fish Finder.

Crazy Crow grabbed her head at the base of the neck and gave it a twist. Not enough to snap Razor Beak's neck, but just enough to let Razor Beak know she would be killed if she did not cooperate.

Razor Beak hissed to frighten her attackers. It was all she could do.

The matriarchs drilled her mind, mining for the memories of her scouting mission with Brown Scale. They found her recollection of Pangea Island.

Flaking Scales recognized the place from legends that circulated among the animals. This was Ghost Island, as the animals called it. It could be seen only when the isle wanted you to see it. Now it made sense why the other scouting parties found only open water.

Fertile Mother suggested they should forget about Brown Scale. If he had gone to Ghost Island, he would no longer be a problem.

Red Eyes disagreed. Brown Scale would be getting most of his food from the sea, which meant he still could come in contact with a female and infect the bloodline with his deformities, and most important of all, his disruptive behavior could upset the hierarchy. Imagine a Flock ruled by males. What would become of the females?

The matriarchs shared her anxiety.

They must follow through on their plan. To Ghost Island they must go. Destroy Brown Scale. Save the bloodline. Save the matriarchy.

17

Brown Scale whiled away the day gliding from cliff to cliff amongst Pangea Island's many mountains. No other animal lived up here. They were down in the valley, under the blanket of mist. Once in a while he heard thrashing in the swamp forest, a gurgling croak from the amphibians. Otherwise it was quiet. The creatures below did not climb up to bother him and he never flew down to bother them. It was perfect harmony.

Being alone was truly beautiful.

It was soothing cool water for the soul.

Peaceful.

The island then spoke to him.

Humans are coming. They want to kill you.

I will kill them first.

Don't. Speak to their leader. You may learn things about the humans which could be useful. The island showed Brown Scale an image of the human who was in charge of the human hunting party. *Speak to him.*

How can I speak to a human? Brown Scale asked.

Bring him to me. I will connect your mind to his so you can talk to each other with your thoughts.

The *Kaga-maru* and her escorts arrived in the area that was photographed by the satellite. As Shindo expected, no island was in sight. Surface radar detected nothing.

But it was out there.

Sayoko stood ready at the fire controls for the laser cannon. The ship was on alert.

As a precaution, Captain Takagi had the escorts and the oiler fall back two kilometers and ordered his entire command to reduce speed to 10 knots.

Impatient, Shindo rechecked the horizon through his binoculars for any crack in the island's façade.

"In about an hour we will reach the point where the satellite took its photos," Captain Takagi said.

"But we should be able to see the island right now, shouldn't we?" Sayoko asked.

The captain nodded.

"Sea bottom is at sixty-five meters," the sonar operator said. He had been giving the depth every five minutes.

"The water is getting shallower," Shindo commented. "Even though we can't see it, it's evident that we're getting close to it."

Captain Takagi chewed his lower lip. His brows were stitched in thought.

Five more minutes elapsed.

"Depth now at fifty-eight meters," the sonar operator said.

Over the next thirty minutes the depth continued to shrink. At the next reading the sonar operator announced that the depth was at twenty meters.

"How shallow does the water need to be before we run aground?" Sayoko asked.

"Eight meters," the captain said.

The ships continued to sail. Another five minutes elapsed.

"Depth still at twenty meters."

The depth remained unchanged at the next reading.

And the next.

Captain Takagi ordered his entire command to slow to five knots.

Shindo could imagine what he was thinking because he was thinking the same thing. If the island could hide from radar it might be able to fool the sonar.

Before the five minutes were up the captain asked for the depth.

"Still at twenty meters."

Shindo heard Captain Takagi mutter under his breath. He could barely hear what the captain said. Something to the order of, "We should be right on top of Pangea by now." Then he shouted, "Full stop! Drop anchor!"

The order came too late. With an unnerving crunch of metal, the ship struck terra firma. The jolt knocked everyone on the bridge off their feet. When they got back up they looked out the bridge windows.

Now Pangea Island could be seen. A beach spread out before the ship, three hundred meters deep. Mountains shot straight up on the far side with steep cliff faces. It was like a fortress of granite, protecting the interior from the outside world. There was no flora or fauna in sight. Nevertheless, the island was alive in ways unparalleled in any other part of the world. This was the land that did not want to be found. It had just granted the crew and passengers of the *Kaga-maru* an audience.

The significance brought a hush over the bridge.

Captain Takagi broke from his reverie first. He issued orders to have the hull inspected for damage and make an assessment on how much effort it was going to take to get them unstuck from the shore.

Before his crew could acknowledge their orders a gigantic winged monster dropped onto the forward deck of the ship. It was brown and black and savage. Its fingers pierced the windows. Glass shards sprayed across the compartment. The monster ripped the top off the bridge as easily as a child peeling the plastic lid off a can of peanuts. It grabbed Shindo and flew into the air.

The monster's grip was not just strong. It was angry. Shindo feared he would be crushed. He was swung up and down as the demon flapped its wings.

Then the flapping stopped. The creature broke into a glide, soared over the peaks, and touched the clouds. The air turned frigid. And then the demon dove at a steep angle. Shindo's guts rose into his throat. His ears popped. The beast hit the ground with a reverberating thud. They arrived in a humid, mist-filled valley. His abductor threw him into the mud along the shore of a lake and then flew away, leaving a wake of swirling fog behind it.

Shindo put his hand on his chest. His heart was beating fast and fierce. He took a deep breath, held it, and then released it slowly. While doing so he focused on the moment. He was on the ground. Alive. Safe.

For the time being.

He recognized the monster. The brown coloring, the armored plating—at long last Shindo found his quarry, and no sooner than he had he was at its mercy. The Flock pterosaur was no longer a juvenile. It was an adult, fifty meters in height, at least. But that didn't worry Shindo as much as the fact the kaiju had singled him out from the others. It was as if the animal knew Shindo had come to kill him.

He rose up on his feet, cautiously, scanning the shoreline for movement. An unearthly silence hung in the air, as thick as the mist. Gradually, his eyes adjusted. He could see trees standing in dense swaths of ferns.

Shaking the mud from his fingers, he drew his sidearm. The back of his hand tingled from a bug crawling across his skin. He looked and found that it wasn't an insect, but a trilobite. It was about the size of a 50-yen coin. The shallow water he was standing in was teeming with them.

Shindo grinned. It was a bit like finding a celebrity. Trilobites were as much a household name as *Tyrannosaurus rex*, at least among paleontologists.

The trilobite lost its grip and dropped back into the water.

Then the mist cleared. Darkness blotted out the sun. Shindo released the safety to his firearm and gripped it with both hands, ready to shoot.

A shaft of light beamed down before him, revealing a massive boulder. Lounging atop it with one forepaw resting over the other was the giant *Dimetrodon*. It looked down at him with its head turned askance.

"What are you?" Shindo asked. "Some say you speak on behalf of the island. Others say you are the island."

The *Dimetrodon* remained stock still.

He heard a question spoken in his head: *Who are you?*

His first reaction was to discount the voice as his imagination, yet he remembered what the legend said. The creature spoke without moving its mouth.

"My name is Yamaguchi, Shindo," Shindo said to the *Dimetrodon*, giving his last name first as per custom.

The *Dimetrodon* did not respond.

"Who's speaking? It's not you, is it?" Shindo pointed at the *Dimetrodon*.

The *Dimetrodon* blinked.

The blink was as clear as spoken words. No, the sail-backed reptile was not the one speaking to him.

"But you are acting as an intermediary, a conduit...translator," Shindo tried to express himself in less complicated terms. "You're linking my mind with someone else's."

The *Dimetrodon* understood. The knowing look in its eye spoke as clearly as the blink. The sail-back was linking Shindo's mind with someone else's, and he had a good idea whose mind it was.

"Then does the one who is speaking to me have a name? My guess is you don't. Being an animal, you probably don't even understand what I am talking about."

Two words came to him: *Brown Scale.*

"Brown Scale," Shindo repeated softly. An apropos name for the brown Flock pterosaur. "Where are you? I can't see you?"

I can see you, Brown Scale replied as though that was enough.

"What do you want with me?"

What do you want with me? Brown Scale sounded as though he already knew and wanted Shindo to condemn himself with his own words.

Clever beast.

Shindo wasn't going to play the kaiju's game.

"If you're sophisticated enough to have a name then you're sophisticated enough to understand why I am here. The question is, what are you going to do about it? I'm at your mercy. You can do anything you want to me."

An invisible force punched its way into Shindo's head and riffled through his private thoughts. His memories played like highlights from a movie.

When the force found what it wanted it withdrew, leaving him feeling violated, his head hurting.

Indifferent to his distress, the *Dimetrodon* blinked. Shindo sensed that the sail-backed reptile had harvested information from his mind and then transmitted it to Brown Scale.

Brown Scale was quiet. He was no doubt taking time to digest what he had been fed.

Shindo waited.

Why do you want to kill me? Brown Scale asked at last.

"Why are you asking? You know."

Brown Scale repeated his question with a firm tone: *Why do you want to kill me?*

"Am I on trial? Is that it?"

Why do you want to kill me?

"Because you are a threat! You killed human beings, creatures like me. You destroyed their homes and property. It's my job to protect them from creatures like you. I confess. I am here to kill you. But you got me first. I await sentence."

You're lying

"Lying? About what?"

The reason why you want to kill me.

"I am not lying. You should know, or don't you trust the information your partner here gave you?" Shindo motioned to the *Dimetrodon*.

You want to kill me because I am different. The words smoldered in Shindo's mind.

"Yes, that's why I consider you a threat."

My Flock mates are a threat. Why aren't you hunting them?

"Because they are not equipped the same way you are. Your body is covered in armor. Theirs aren't. You have an opposable thumb and an aptitude for using tools. They don't. You are better than them. You're an improvement."

I am better than them? A cackling sound echoed throughout the valley. It was raspy, just what one would expect from the throat of a reptile.

"Yes," Shindo stressed. "I doubt you will understand, but you are a product of adaptive evolution. Your kind has been fighting my kind for so long it is developing traits that will increase its chances of survival. You are the first to be born with these traits. Once you mate, those traits can be passed on to the next generation. Within a few years my kind could be facing hundreds of creatures like you. We won't be able to contain you. You will overrun us. We will face extinction."

A fresh round of cackling echoed overhead.

I will not mate. I want nothing to do with my kind. I don't want anything to do with anyone. I like being alone.

Shindo was taken aback. He never would have imagined that Brown Scale, this advancement in adaptive evolution, could also be an evolutionary dead end.

"You don't want to mate?"

No.

Brown Scale's sincerity was still sound.

"What are you going to do when mating season comes? How are you going to stop yourself from seeking a mate?"

You don't understand because you don't know how good it feels to be alone.

Shindo listened carefully and could find no hint of trickery. The monster's attitude was of one who was secure enough in his position that he had no need to lie. So it appeared that Shindo's fears about Brown Scale were unfounded. Nevertheless, there was something not right about Brown Scale.

Shindo looked for a way out of here. Behind him was the lake. The shore was unguarded, but how far would he get before his hosts stopped him?

This meeting seemed to have been arranged for Brown Scale's benefit. Perhaps if he convinced Brown Scale there was no point in holding him, he might be allowed to return to the ship. The thing he had to take into account was that the *Dimetrodon* was reading his mind on Brown Scale's behalf. Negotiating with this creature was going to be like playing Poker with his cards exposed on the table.

"If this is true," Shindo said, "then you're not a threat. I have no reason to be here. Will you let me go?"

I will have to kill you. You don't believe me.

"Of course not. Even if you don't think you'll ever mate, the possibility is still there. As we humans like to say, you never know who you're going to meet. That special someone can be just around the corner and before you know it you're a dad with a nest full of eggs."

You don't understand.

"You're right. I don't. Help me."

Brown Scale became quiet.

Shindo could sense that his thoughts were being carefully examined.

It won't matter if I convince you. You won't change your mind about killing me.

"That's because I can't change my mind. Only you can. If you want to be left alone by my kind, this is your chance to make that happen."

Something started stirring within Brown Scale. Shindo braced himself. He might have asked for more than he had anticipated.

And he was right.

Brown Scale passed his memories to the *Dimetrodon*. The *Dimetrodon* pushed the memories into Shindo's mind. Shindo found himself seeing the world through Brown Scale's eyes from when he was an infant. He heard the adults screeching about Brown Scale's appearance. They thought Brown Scale was deformed. The Flock's leader ordered his mother to kill him. She pulled him out of the nest, dropped him on the ground and started stabbing him with her beak. Shindo found out what it felt like to be the victim of an attempted murder. He felt the blows to Brown Scale's back. He experienced terror, bewilderment, and rejection.

After stabbing didn't work, Brown Scale's mother grabbed him and tried to snap his neck by shaking him. Brown Scale's fear turned into anger and he attacked his mother, clawing her eye. He then attacked the leader. His father pulled him away and set him down. The adults left him alone, but Brown Scale's ordeal was just beginning. His mother refused to keep him warm at night. She refused to feed him. He lay in the nest, unwelcomed, cold, hungry, and helpless. He nearly starved until his father brought him food. Since then Brown Scale looked forward to the day when he could fend for himself, so he would not have to rely on anyone else. He yearned to be alone with the same intensity another person would long for company. The idea of becoming physically intimate with his own kind filled him with revulsion. It was impossible for him to mate.

Now Shindo understood.

The *Dimetrodon* broke the psychic link between Shindo and Brown Scale.

Like the mud on his clothes, the kaiju's memories left their stain. They were hard to shake.

They felt so real that they seemed like his memories rather than those of another.

"Tell Brown Scale I'm sorry," Shindo said. "I was wrong. If you let me go I will tell my people to leave him alone. We will not come to these waters again."

The *Dimetrodon* blinked.

Shindo vanished from the island and reappeared in his quarters aboard the ship.

He put his hand to his chest and took a deep breath in relief.

Shindo sensed Pangea's presence in the room. It was waiting to see if he would keep his word. He could sense it. There was also no telling how long the island was going to wait.

He ran up to the bridge. The open ceiling was letting the sea air flow freely through the compartment. Everyone was shocked to see him.

"Shindo!" Yomo grabbed the sides of his arms. A big grin was on his partner's face. "What happened? How did you get back on board?"

"How long was I gone?"

"Twenty minutes, or so. Tell us what happened."

"Later." Shindo pulled himself free and stepped up to the captain. "Will you be able to free the ship?"

"No. I'm making arrangements to disperse the crew to the other ships. I'll lend you a security detail to help protect the laser cannon. What are you going to do?"

"I'm going to send a message to my chief and see if I can get the mission aborted."

"Abort?" Takagi's brows shot up.

"We can't abort!" Sayoko exclaimed. "We came here to kill the armored pterosaur."

"We're not going to kill him," Shindo said.

"We're going to have to use the cannon to kill something! I can't go back without any results. How is my company going to sell more units?"

Yomo motioned to his wife to calm down.

"The armored pterosaur is not a threat," Shindo said. "His name is Brown Scale. I spoke to him. Telepathically. He won't mate with his own kind. He's sort of a…" He fumbled for the right words. "He's sort of a recluse. I'll explain once we're on our way. Right now we need to head home as soon as possible. I suspect the island allowed us to find it for a purpose and that purpose has been served. At this point it's anyone's guess what the island is going to do. The sooner we pull out the better."

"What about the laser cannon?" Sayoko asked.

"We can try salvaging it," Takagi said. "We'll have to disassemble it piece by piece. It'll take a day or so to get the job done."

"No," Shindo countered. "Too long. It'll have to be destroyed as per security protocol."

Sayoko dropped her jaw.

Before round two could get into full swing, Yomo called everyone's attention to the beach. Brown Scale came down for a landing, stirring up a cloud of sand around him. He was an incredible sight compared to his photos. A typical Flock member was sleek, and elegant. Brown Scale's armor made him look husky, like a medieval warrior. One could not help feeling threatened by his presence.

Shindo stepped forward so the kaiju could see him clearly. They made eye contact. When Brown Scale was certain Shindo had changed his mind, he ambled toward the ship. The crew out on the deck aimed their weapons at him.

Captain Takagi shouted at them to stand down.

Brown Scale kept coming, unconcerned about the guns.

"You better tell your men to get inside," Shindo said to the captain.

Takagi nodded and called out to his crew to clear the deck and then got on the intercom to warn everyone to brace themselves.

Brown Scale grabbed the destroyer's prow and shoved the warship back out into deeper water. The bridge crew cheered. Captain Takagi issued the order to power up the turbines. His men cheered even louder. They were going home. Sayoko put her hand to her chest, breathless with relief. Her gun was saved.

The *Kaga-maru* turned around. All the while the kaiju pterosaur watched them from the front porch of his home, so to speak. Shindo could not image Brown Scale ever leaving this island. He watched Brown Scale watching them. Like the island, he would probably never see Brown Scale again.

As the ship completed its turn storm clouds darkened the sky. Lightning flickered. Thunder rumbled deep inside the weather front's throat. An icy breeze picked up speed. There was an unhealthy aspect to this storm. Evil.

"Captain," Takagi's communications officer spoke, "we received a message from our oiler. Their sonar detected an object approaching from astern. It's over a hundred fifty meters long with an estimated weight of 25,000 tons."

"Did Tylogon follow us?" Yomo wondered out loud.

An arc of lightning flashed overhead. Thunder growled.

In the next moment a plasma ray beam pierced the replenishment oiler from under the surface of the sea. The ship exploded. Smoke billowed into the bruised sky. Then up from the water rose the mutant theropod that both man and beast feared so much. Tiamatodon had arrived.

18

White Sail found Razor Beak on the beach trying to put her dislocated wing finger back in place. Razor Beak felt embarrassed and didn't want her mother's help. Dislocating wing fingers is what juveniles did. Not adults. Regardless, White Sail was her mother. She was going to help her daughter whether she wanted it or not.

White Sail landed at the bottom of the ridge, selected a boulder with a flat surface, and rolled it over to Razor Beak. When she got close, she saw claw marks. Her grownup offspring had been attacked. There were foot prints all around, large ones. They could only have been made by the matriarchs.

Razor Beak avoided eye contact with her mother and tried to shuffle away so she could fix her finger herself.

White Sail cooed at her to calm her and gently clamped onto Razor Beak's neck so she could pull her over to the stone. Razor Beak was in too much pain to pull away. White Sail placed the injured hand atop the flat boulder.

Razor Beak became scared.

White Sail kept cooing a Flock lullaby and gripped Razor Beak's forearm, bracing it. Pulling her other wing back, she summoned all of her strength and slammed the heel of her palm down on the finger joint. It snapped back in place with a loud crack.

Razor Beak wailed and fluttered across the beach like a wounded butterfly. The initial shock ran its course. She laid on her side, holding her sore hand, panting heavily.

Peeps landed on the beach to see what the commotion was about.

White Sail loomed over her daughter and chirped at her, asking who attacked her.

Razor Beak clucked, *The matriarchs.*

They flew away a while ago, Peeps said telepathically. *That way.* She turned her head toward the west.

White Sail was puzzled. Nothing was out that way. She and Yellow Claws had searched those waters. She asked Razor Beak why the matriarchs had attacked her.

Razor Beak showed White Sail her memories of Pangea Island.

White Sail prodded her to continue. The matriarchs must have wanted more than just the location of an island.

Razor Beak croaked, *Brown Scale.*

White Sail pieced together the puzzle from her daughter's fragmented thoughts. Brown Scale had flown to the island and the matriarchs were on their way to kill him.

19

The rules of engagement with kaiju did not apply to Tiamatodon. The Siamese-twin was going to attack. It always attacked. The only viable response was to attack first, hit hard, and pray. The Japanese Maritime Defense sailors rushed to battle stations.

Sayoko lowered her targeting goggles over her eyes and brought the laser cannon's controls online.

The armorer distributed assault rifles and raincoats to the crew and a light machine gun to Shindo. A security detail armed with anti-tank rockets joined them. With the roof ripped open, the bridge was ostensibly an exposed position.

The very thing Goro had warned Shindo could happen had happened. Tiamatodon found him, and he was stuck on a ship where his skills would not be of any use and there was no escape.

Nevertheless, Shindo kept his faith that he would still be able to make a difference. Life was fluid. Hope had a way of cropping up in the midst of hopelessness.

Takagi ordered his command to commence attack. The frigates *Nakajima* and *Tanaka* dropped floating smoke canisters in Tiamatodon's path to block its line of sight. Once the smoke masked the monster's view of the ships, Takagi's command launched torpedoes and missiles. The frigates pelted the twin-headed kaiju with additional fire from their 76mm cannons. Explosions flashed within the smoke cloud. The rippling cannonade blended with the storm's thunder.

Sayoko depressed the trigger to the laser cannon. The laser's silvery red beam pierced the smoke screen.

Shindo watched the assault on her fire control's screen. He could see what she was seeing through her thermal imager. The beam struck the creature in the chest, right over the heart.

Tiamatodon continued to advance with the laser beam sizzling against its chest. It stepped out of the smoke screen, seemingly unaffected. Then it reeled, screaming in fury.

"We hurt him!" Yomo shouted. "We actually hurt him!"

Captain Takagi showed his relief for a moment with a smile. Through his COMMO he ordered his escorts to withdraw and then gave orders to his own ship to go around the monster.

Hope was becoming tangible, and exhilarating. They were holding at bay a beast that could summon storms like a god.

Then their opponent drew lightning from the sky.

Yomo clutched his wife's shoulder. "This is it."

The monster was brewing up to fire its plasma rays. The destroyer's hull would not be able to withstand the rays any better than the oiler.

Sayoko raised her sights from the chest to the heads. The wound she had scored on Tiamatodon's chest smoked like a cigarette burn. It looked like the *Heartbreaker* was not going to have much effect. Sayoko depressed the trigger. Her beam struck the female half. Tiamatodon took half a step back. Its female head turned away, squinting from the laser beam's glare. The female half wanted to retreat, but the male half refused. He drew in his breath, getting ready to fire.

Sayoko swung her laser beam into the male's face. It was no use. He was too committed to be dissuaded by the laser.

The male half fired his plasma rays—and his shot missed. The plasma beam struck the sea. At the instant Tiamatodon exhaled his rays Brown Scale rammed into the male half with his chest keel. The bone on bone impact resulted in a loud crack.

Takagi looked at Tiamatodon through his binoculars. "Brown Scale drew blood."

Shindo looked through his binoculars. He saw a chink in the male head's shiny black scales and a wet dollop of red around the wound. This was the first time anyone or any creature had ever punctured Tiamatodon's tough hide.

Brown Scale swung high up into the air and looped around for another dive.

Lightning bolts flashed around him, silhouetting him as they arced down to the spines on Tiamatodon's back. Sayoko fired a jolt at one head and then the other to throw off Tiamatodon's aim.

"Come on, Brown Scale," Yomo muttered. His fists were clenched. "Tiamatodon's just standing there. Nail him good!"

As Brown Scale neared his target five other Flock pterosaurs intercepted him. They were females. Shindo could tell by the sharp points of their sail rods. One of them had red scales around her eyes. That one rammed into Brown Scale with her keel. He spun out of control and splashed into the water behind Tiamatodon.

Tiamatodon built up its charge for a fresh attack, but instead of firing plasma rays, it banked the charge and spun around and slammed its tail into the sea. A wall of water fell upon the *Kaga-maru*, dousing the laser beam. Water also splashed inside the bridge, shorting out Sayoko's controls.

The laser turret sat quiet. Steam curled from its heated surface.

Sayoko's fingers scrambled across the keys of the controls, pulled plugs and reinserted them. The controls were dead. There was no getting around it.

Sayoko popped the targeting goggles up from her eyes. "I'm going to need my laptop. It's down in my quarters."

"It's too late," Yomo lamented.

Tiamatodon inhaled, getting ready to spew its plasma beams.

"Keep him busy." Shindo shoved the light machine gun into his partner's arms. "I'll get the laptop."

Sayoko threw Shindo the keys to her quarters as he exited the bridge.

After Tiamatodon completed its spin, its tail swept within Brown Scale's reach. Brown Scale grabbed it, climbed up Tiamatodon's back, and leapt into the air. His leap inadvertently pushed Tiamatodon forward just when it fired its plasma rays. The rays fell short again, striking the water off the *Kaga's* starboard side.

Tiamatodon had its aim thrown twice. Enraged, the twin-headed beast roared up at Brown Scale.

Brown Scale pumped his wings to gain speed and altitude.

The matriarchs swooped in for a second attack. Fish Finder cawed to Red Eyes, asking for the honor to strike next. Red Eyes granted her request with a staccato chitter. The matriarch formation flew head-on toward Brown Scale.

Brown Scale maintained course. Fish Finder was in his path. The two flying reptiles measured each other up for weaknesses. The elder of the two was cemented in her confidence that she would be the victor. Within the moment they were about to clash, Brown Scale banked to the left, nearly colliding with Stoop Shoulders. Stoop Shoulders squawked. Fish Finder adjusted her course, but she was too late. Brown Scale had slipped through the formation unscathed.

Without missing a beat, he finished his loop and dived toward Tiamatodon.

Shindo returned from Sayoko's quarters with her laptop in hand. Sayoko grabbed it and mounted it to the fire control pedestal.

As she rushed to get the laser turret back online, Tiamatodon drew a fresh bolt of lightning to recharge its plasma rays. The *Kaga* launched the last of her missiles in an effort to forestall the kaiju long enough to escape.

Yomo watched Brown Scale coming in for another dive and shook his head. "There is no way we are going to get lucky a third time."

Tiamatodon drew in its breath and exhaled, spewing its rays. Brown Scale landed on its back in the same breath. The beams went wild again, but not wild enough to miss the ship's mast. It softened to the consistency of liquid wax and drained down the sides of the ship.

Captain Takagi ordered his command to hold fire lest they hit their benefactor.

Brown Scale clung to Tiamatodon's back and pecked the two heads. Tiamatodon thrashed about, trying to fling him off. Brown Scale countered by using Tiamatodon's spines as hand holds.

"He's buying us time," Shindo said to Takagi.

The captain regarded him wryly. "How long do you think he can hold out? Tiamatodon is three times his size."

Shindo didn't want to think about it.

Sayoko got the laser turret back online and opened fire at Tiamatodon's belly.

The *Nakajima* and *Tanaka* had sailed far enough away from the battle to escape the monsters' notice. As per Takagi's orders they kept sailing. It was up to the *Kaga* to get clear. She plied the waves at 30 knots, her top speed. Yet, it seemed as though she were slithering at a snail's pace.

Tiamtodon bludgeoned Brown Scale with its tail. He refused to let go. So long as he held on, the Two-Headed One would be preoccupied with him. It was vital that the humans escape so they could convince their leaders to leave him alone. Brown Scale valued his solitude that much.

Overhead, the matriarchs circled. They watched to see if he would lose his grip.

Out of defiance to them, Brown Scale bore up to the assault.

Eventually, the ship sailed past Tiamatodon. Sayoko let up on the trigger to the laser cannon once the two-headed kaiju was out of the gun's arc of fire.

Shindo and Yomo went out onto the bridge wing to see how well Brown Scale was faring.

"Do you think he was buying us time?" Yomo asked. "Or was he just defending his territory."

"Both, I imagine," Shindo said. "I have a promise to keep. I hope he lives long enough to benefit from it."

20

With the ship safe, Brown Scale switched his focus on the matriarchs. He took off from Tiamatodon's back, flew through the storm clouds and up into the clear sky. The sun was bright and cheerful above him while below the cloud deck flickered with ominous light.

As expected the matriarchs followed him through the deck. He ambushed Stooped Shoulders. His keel opened her skin in a straight line, cutting at an angle between the shoulder blades. Her brittle bones snapped. She yelped in anguish and fell like a broken kite into the clouds.

Red Eyes hissed venomously at the loss.

Brown Scale dived through the cloud deck to the storm underneath.

Stooped Shoulders splashed in the sea just as he passed through the clouds. She flailed in the water. His strike had severed several of her back muscles. It would not be long before she sank.

The other matriarchs would not fall for the same trick twice. He flew toward the mountains.

On the way a Flock keel struck him in the back and a glob of drool dropped into his eye. His armor held as it did before. Yet the impact spun him out of control. He stiffened his arms so his wings worked as airbrakes against the spin. Regaining control, he searched for his assailant with his good eye. He couldn't see her, but an inarticulate caw called out behind him.

Crazy Crow.

She had played the same trick on him as he had on her comrades.

Brown Scale heard the leathery flap of her wings as she flew back up into the storm clouds. He dove for terra firma, toward the mountains, where he knew every ambush point and they did not.

At the mountains, he clung to the sheer cliff face overlooking the beach. There he wiped the phlegm from his eye and looked back over the sea. Tiamatodon was marching toward the shore. The matriarchs were nowhere in sight.

Did he dare switch opponents?

The island's fauna would be powerless against the Two-Headed One.

Then he sensed the island's mental energy at work. It gathered water at the beach. The salty fluid piled up in a mound standing two hundred meters at its summit. In one psychic push, the island shoved the water toward Tiamatodon.

Tiamatodon stopped and bowed its heads in concentration. The behemoth threw up a psychic barrier. The wave smashed against the invisible shield and drained around Tiamatodon.

Brown Scale felt feeble after witnessing such a display of power.

Yet, if he were to save his home, he would have to join the battle…which was exactly what the matriarchs wanted.

Now he understood why they had not shown themselves. They were holding back until he engaged the Two-Headed One. They had fought this creature before. They knew how dangerous it was.

Nevertheless, his home meant everything to him. He might never find another like it.

Brown Scale waited for the right moment to strike.

Tiamatodon marched onto the beach. The ground shook under its footfalls.

The island made a second attempt to stop the beast by enveloping it in a cloud of yellow gas. The gas seeped from the sand. Brown Scale could tell by its sickly color it was toxic. Tiamatodon's foot falls continued several more steps then stopped and changed to thrashing about with the tail thumping the ground. Choking sounds came from the fog.

In response, Tiamatodon summoned gale-force winds to blow away the gas. Brown Scale got a whiff of the vapor as the tempest dispelled it. It was noxious like rotten eggs.

Tiamatodon resumed its march, heading for a pass between the mountains. The wind buffeted the sea while the thunder hammered its anvils.

Brown Scale pushed away from the cliff and took flight. The wind resisted him, making his sore arms work harder. He circled around behind

Tiamatodon. Before he attacked, he checked for the matriarchs. They were still nowhere to be seen. His instincts warned him that they were close. Yet, so long as they were not visible, they should not be near enough to ambush him.

He attacked.

With the wind now on his back, he picked up more velocity for this next dive.

Tiamatodon paused, turned one of its heads and spotted Brown Scale.

Brown Scale picked up speed just in case he could bring his keel to bare before the twin-headed kaiju could make a countermove.

It was no use. Tiamatodon spun around, swinging its tail like a club. Despite the monster's bulk, it pirouetted too swiftly. Its tail was a black blur of motion.

Brown Scale broke his attack, flapped his wings, once, and whooshed over Tiamatodon and into the mountain pass. The swinging tail missed him by mere meters.

As he flew down the narrow passage, Brown Scale plotted his next move. While he did so Red Eyes, Fish Finder, and Fertile Mother entered the pass from the opposite end, heading toward him. Fish Finder flew directly at him with the intent of making a second attempt at striking him with her keel. Fertile Mother flew below her and Red Eyes flew above her so they could intercept him if he tried to outmaneuver Fish Finder. The three matriarchs screeched with glee. The passage did not afford enough room to bank off to the side. He would have to either fly above Fish Finder and be attacked by Red Eyes or fly below her and be attacked by Fertile Mother.

Brown Scale lowered his head sail and looked behind him, expecting to see Flaking Scales and Crazy

Crow closing the trap from behind. He found Flaking Scales, but she didn't enter the pass from behind. She was dropping straight down into the pass from the cloud deck, heel's first. Flaking Scales had planned her attack perfectly. She would land on his back and smash him into the rocks below, unless he slowed down. In which case, she would miss him, but then he would be an easy mark for Fish Finder. She would be able to strike him with her keel with precision and aim for the unarmored parts of his body.

Brown Scale acted fast. He twisted his axis from the horizontal to the vertical. Flaking Scales swooshed past him and landed on the rocks below. She cawed in disgust. Red Eyes, Fish Finder, and Fertile Mother had no choice but match his axis or risk crashing into him and falling to the ground in a heap of broken wings.

Now he had plenty of room to maneuver. Using the same tactic as last time, he banked around Fish Finder. The three matriarchs squawked at the injustice and then cawed in panic when they found themselves speeding toward Tiamatodon.

Brown Scale exited the passage and glided over the mist-filled valley. The winds had yet to penetrate this sanctuary, although the thunder rumbled overhead. He could sense the island concentrating on Tiamatodon. It was preparing a new attack. His instinct told him to be careful. The island was going to do something big.

He flew toward the mountain peaks and into the low, flickering clouds. As he crested the peak he heard a leathery flap of wings. His senses went on full alert, but the clouds masked his attacker's approach.

It was Crazy Crow.

Again.

He had forgotten her.

Again.

Crazy Crow grabbed his right wing finger in her beak.

Out of reflex, he wrenched his finger free before she could snap it. He fell and tumbled down the mountain slope, down below the clouds. No sooner had he regained his footing, Crazy Crow pounced on him, sending him skidding further down the slope in a cascade of rocks and dust.

When he stopped tumbling, he got back up on all fours as quickly as he could and searched for Crazy Crow.

She was further up the slope, cackling. The eccentric kaiju dropped her 4,500 tons of weight upon a boulder, dislodging it. The murderous rock rolled down toward Brown Scale, picking up speed.

Brown Scale leapt into the air. The boulder smashed his perch amongst the cliffs and continued down to the beach.

With his wing finger hurt, each flap sent a stinging sensation down his arm. His speed diminished. His concentration divided between the pain and his opponents.

Red Eyes struck him from behind with her keel. His armor held. Nevertheless, his momentum slowed further. He lost altitude. And he lost more speed and altitude when Fertile Mother struck him and then Fish Finder. Fish Finder cawed with joy in finally scoring a hit.

Out of desperation he pumped his arms harder, faster. The matriarchs were driving him toward Tiamatodon.

The behemoth stopped its march at the mouth of the pass and turned to face him. It drew a charge of lightning from the storm. The flash of light blinded Brown Scale. Thunder shocked his ears. He tried to change course and escape, but his injured eyes did not recover in time from the lightning flash. He flew within Tiamatodon's reach. The male half of the monster grabbed Brown Scale in its jaws. Brown Scale flapped wildly. He squawked in panic.

The matriarchs gathered up on the slope and like vultures they waited to see if Brown Scale would die.

The male half of the monster bit down on Brown Scale. Memories of his mother biting down on him when he was a hatchling flashed in his mind's eye. When Tiamatodon couldn't crush his armor, it swung him around, just like his mother, and then threw him down onto the granite slope leading up to the pass. It stomped on Brown Scale's chest. His keel lodged into the thick tissue padding Tiamatodon's foot. Annoyed, Tiamatodon growled. It shook its foot until the keel came loose. Brown Scale flopped onto his back. The old hate and anger that burned inside him on the day of his birth came back. Quickly, he rolled over, took flight, rebounded off the slope and came right back, aiming to strike the wound he had already opened on Tiamatodon's head. Tiamatodon reacted with unanticipated speed. The male half blasted Brown Scale in the chest with his plasma ray. The beam slammed Brown Scale into the slope. The female half followed up with a second blow. The energy burst hit Brown Scale with so much force it brought an avalanche down upon him.

The matriarchs squealed with delight. Flaking Scales descended from her perch to get a close look at the mess. She flapped, holding her place in the air, behind Tiamatodon.

The dust settled, and there was no mess to be seen.

Brown Scale survived. His armor withstood Tiamatodon's rays.

Flaking Scales squawked.

Nothing had ever withstood a blast from Tiamatodon. Nothing!

Brown Scale was as shocked as Flaking Scales. But now that he knew his armor would give him a fighting chance he rose up. Rocks and dust slid off of his body. He unleashed an ear-piercing shriek at Tiamatodon. The cry told the Two-Headed One it had met its equal.

Tiamatodon spread its feet and thumped the ground with its tail. It yelled out in its withering double roar. The Two-Headed One was ready for him.

Then the earth shook. A horrible rumbling from within the island drowned out the thunder. Steam spouted from the cracks in the granite slope. Then the floor of the pass swelled, filling the gap between the mountains. Lava burst from the swelled earth and rushed down the slope.

Tiamtodon lowered its heads in concentration. It threw up its psychic barrier. The lava smashed through it and swept the mutant kaiju down the beach.

Brown Scale took off to escape the falling ash and toxic gas.

The matriarchs swooped down after him. Soon the flying reptiles engaged in an aerial ballet above the oozing rock. Swooping, diving, feinting and dodging, the two sides tried to cut each other with their keels. The matriarchs had the edge. They only needed to avoid one keel—his—while Brown Scale had to avoid all of theirs. His youth allowed him to keep up, for now, but he would tire first and the one who tired was the one who lost. The matriarchs were wise old fighters. Each time Brown Scale attempted to dart into the mountains, they intercepted him, kept him out in the open where he was at a disadvantage.

Below, Tiamatodon thrashed in the lava until the island buried it in molten rock. The rock glowed with a raging color of orange. The storm that Tiamatodon had summoned did not cease, though. Instead the wind and rain intensified. The temperature dropped to near freezing.

Flying became impossible.

Brown scale landed on the beach five hundred meters from where the island had the Two-Headed One entombed in lava.

The matriarchs landed between him and the sea. The steep mountain slopes were at his back. Despite their age, the matriarchs still had yet another advantage over him. They were each ten to fifteen meters taller and several tons heavier. It was going to be easier for them to wield their beaks and claws against him.

Brown Scale hissed, raising his head sail in a threatening display.

Flaking Scales faced him. Her fellow matriarchs slowly spread out in a circle around him.

What did you do to Razor Beak? Brown Scale demanded, communicating with telepathy. *She was the only one who knew I could be found here. She never would have told you willing.*

Flaking Scales cut his mind off to him. He was a nonentity to her, now. All he was to her was that deformed hatchling she wanted to kill so long ago.

Red Eyes and Fertile Mother fanned out from Flaking Scale's left. Fish Finder fanned out from her right.

But where was Crazy Crow?

Brown Scale was not going to attack first until he knew where the crazy matriarch was hiding.

As he searched for her, he spotted a Flock pterosaur dropping from the sky. She landed between him and Flaking Scales.

It was White Sail, his mother.

Peeps landed beside him. She hissed at the matriarchs, daring them to attack.

Flaking Scales gave White Sail a cautionary hiss, raising her head sail part way.

White Sail hissed back, raising her sail all the way.

Forget about your deformed offspring, Flaking Scales chittered to White Sail. *You are young. You can hatch many more eggs.*

White Sail replied with another hiss.

You are making the mistake many first time mothers make, Flaking Scales cawed. *You are too attached to your first batch of offspring. The others learned to let go. Let go, White Sail. Let go!*

White Sail took a step toward Flaking Scales.

Red Eyes hissed at Brown Scale's mother. She raised her head sail in warning.

Look at your unmated daughter, Flaking Scales chittered. *She guards her brother as though he were her offspring. She doesn't understand the threat he poses to the bloodline. Kill them both and start over.*

White Sail took another step forward.

Flaking Scales was not intimidated. She had a twelve meter height advantage over White Sail. *Brown Scale scarred your right eye,* she reminded White Sail. *No offspring that strikes its mother shall live!*

My son attacked because you told me to kill him, White Sail replied with a drawn out, throaty hiss. *You cost me my right eye.*

White Sail charged Flaking Scales. Flaking Scales lunged with her beak in an attempt to grab Brown Scale's mother by the throat. White Sail blocked her attempt with her wing. The matriarch's beak clamped down on White Sail's forearm. White Sail hopped up above Flaking Scales' head and shoved her arm deeper into the matriarch's mouth in order to dislocate her jaw. Before she could press her advantage, Flaking Scales shoved her back and released her arm. The two females hissed at each other.

While Flaking Scales and White Sail fought, Red Eyes cawed, ordering the matriarchs to charge Brown Scale and Peeps.

The elder females were going to use height and weight to gain the advantage. Flying was not an option in this wind. The best move would be to do the opposite. Go low. Brown Scale charged Red Eyes, the Old Ones' leader. As she rose up on her hind legs to bring her claws to bare he dove for the ground, grabbing her ankle into his mouth and scrambled underneath her. Red Eyes fell onto the beach. Peeps hopped on top of her and shredded Red Eyes' wings with her claws. Red Eyes wailed. Fertile Mother and Fish Finder ripped into Peeps with their claws. Peeps snapped at Fertile Mother with her beak. Fertile Mother pulled back. While Peeps had her neck extended, Fish Finder grabbed her throat in her beak.

Brown Scale released Red Eyes' ankle and grabbed Fish Finder's neck with his beak.

As the claws and beaks drew blood, the wind and rain cooled the molten rock. Cracks formed in the hardened lava. They multiplied and spread, causing the lava to crumble. The Flock pterosaurs failed to notice what was happening until it was too late. Tiamatodon pushed itself up from the rock. Both heads roared.

Brown Scale released Fish Finder and gawked in disbelief.

Fertile Mother disentangled herself from the melee and took off for the mountains.

Tiamatodon blasted her with its plasma ray. Brown Scale caught a whiff of burnt meat in the wind as her blackened body arced through the sky and smacked the rock face of a cliff with a sickening splat.

Fish Finder wrenched Peep's neck in attempt to snap it before she fled. Peeps rolled with the twist and raked Fish Finder's throat with her claws, getting one of her claws hooked in the loose skin.

There was no way Fish Finder was going to be able to kill her adversary before Tiamatodon destroyed them both. She took off, flapping in desperation. However, Peep's finger was still caught in Fish Finder's skin. The matriarch dragged the young adult female with her for several meters before Peep's claw ripped through the skin. They both sprawled across the beach. Peeps crawled after Fish Finder to get a second purchase on her. Fish Finder was up on all fours before Peeps could reach her. The matriarch also inadvertently made herself the priority target. As soon as she spread her wings Tiamatodon fired its plasma ray. The beam blasted her to bits.

Brown Scale cawed at Peeps to follow him. They flapped toward another pass in the mountains.

Red Eyes got back up. Her wings shredded, she could no longer fly. The Old One did what she could. She honored her station as matriarch by keeping her dignity and hissed at Tiamatodon. She raised her head sail to signal that she was still a threat.

Both of Tiamatodon's heads spewed plasma beams at her. The rays swept her up like the wind and sent her rolling down the beach. When Tiamatodon let up, there was nothing left that could be recognized as Red Eyes.

Brown Scale and Peeps hid in the mountain pass. They saw Tiamatodon turn toward their mother and Flaking Scales. White Sail and the grand matriarch were too intent on killing each other to notice that they were the Two-Headed One's next target.

Brown Scale and Peeps burst from the pass and soared down the beach and before the monster could draw fresh lightning from the sky, Brown Scale clung to its chest and Peeps clung to its side. There was something odd about its black scales. They were squishy. The lava had not killed Tiamatodon, but it had softened its thick hide. Brown Scale pecked once and got his beak stuck in one of the kaiju's throats.

Tiamatodon was as surprised as Brown Scale and Peeps. The flying reptiles now had the advantage. As quickly as possible they scratched Tiamatodon's abdomen with the claws on their feet, stripping layers of dermal tissue. Before they could expose any muscle or vital organs, Tiamatodon counterattacked. It looped its tail around Brown Scale's neck and ripped him from its chest with a fistful of jelly in each hand. The male head grabbed Peeps with his jaws and threw her to the ground. Tiamatodon stomped on her. Her ribs snapped. It then slammed Brown Scale onto the hardened lava.

Brown Scale blacked out.

When he came to, the wind and rain had ceased. The clouds were breaking up. Tiamatodon was gone. Its tracks showed where it had retreated back into the sea.

Peeps lay near the tracks. Her eyes were half open. Her torso had been crushed. Peeps was dead.

White Sail was cawing for him and his sister.

Brown Scale flew to her. She was standing over Flaking Scales on the shore. Flaking Scales was dead. His mother had fought hard for her victory. She bled from many cuts. The delicate pteroid bone on her right wrist had been snapped and the wing membrane that it was attached to above the arm was torn. Brown Scale examined the grand matriarch. Her dead eye stared up at him. He flipped her limp head over with his beak. Her other eye was slashed by claw marks.

White Sail chittered proudly. The score was even.

She then told him to fly Flaking Scales out into the shallow water where the tide could carry her away.

The body was terribly heavy, but once it sank out of sight Brown Scale felt free. Truly free.

He returned to his mother and pressed his forehead to hers to show her what happened to Peeps. He faced the direction of where she lay.

White Sail limped to her daughter. She didn't fly. The broken pteroid bone was causing her a lot of pain.

Closing her eyes, White Sail hunched over Peeps and uttered soft, chittering sounds in her throat just as she had done with her brother's bones. Brown Scale followed suit. He now understood how his mother felt when she mourned for her brother.

Bury her, White Sail clucked, *so the scavengers can't scatter her bones.*

Brown Scale deposited his sister in the pass where they had hid and brought the rocks down from the slopes, covering her.

His mother had flown away. He found her on the highest cliff facing east, toward his old home. The swelling around her right wrist had worsened. When the wind pushed against her, she winced.

White Sail announced that she was going back to the Flock.

Brown Scale told her to wait until her wrist healed.

White Sail looked at him for a long time to get a lasting memory of him to take with her. She looked at him in the way she should have when he was a hatchling. Nevertheless, her loving gaze healed an old, old wound. The past lost its sting.

An offspring shouldn't see its mother suffer, White Sail clucked. She leapt from the cliff with her wings outstretched and plummeted toward the rocks below. When it looked like she was going to smash against the stones, she looped up into the air and reached a height higher than the mountains. After a couple of unsteady flaps she leveled off into a smooth glide. Despite her aching wrist, she made flying look majestic.

Brown Scale watched her as she entered the clouds. When the clouds passed, she was no longer in sight. He remained where he was to stretch out the moment. In time the moment left him and there was no more reason to stay.

White Sail was gone.

He sensed someone watching him. Brown Scale turned and found Crazy Crow perched atop the ridge. She had the remains of Fertile Mother in her beak. Or was it Red Eyes? It was hard to tell. She dropped the burnt meat and held it down so it wouldn't roll away.

It's tough being different, Crazy Crow told him with telepathy.

If she were the same as the other Flock pterosaurs, her mental faculties should have weakened because there was just the two of them, but they didn't. Her faculties remained strong like his.

At least the thing that made me different was not as obvious as the thing that made you different, Crazy Crow said in regard to his armored plates and extra finger. She glanced down at the burnt meat. *I told Red Eyes we should've waited. The Two-Headed One was coming. I saw it in my mind. I saw it!*

Crazy Crow scowled at him and then let the matter drop. *At least I got a free lunch out of it.* She ripped a hunk of meat off the corpse and swallowed it. The Old One then stared at him. *Do you trust me?*

No, Brown Scale replied telepathically. *But I can tell you don't want to kill me anymore.*

Crazy Crow nodded in satisfaction. She ripped a few more strips of meat off the corpse she had called a "free lunch", swallowed them, and then said, *Congratulations. Your enemies are dead and you are alive. That makes you the victor.* She picked up her meal and placed it before Brown Scale as an offering and flew away.

21

Upon returning to Japan, Shindo filed his report with Goro Yamashita, who passed it up to the defense minister. Two days later the prime minister called Shindo to The Château where he and his advisors questioned Shindo on his report.

"Do you stand by your assertion that the armored Flock pterosaur—Brown Scale—is not a threat?"

"Yes."

"What changed your mind?"

Shindo repeated what he had stated in his report verbatim. The prime minister and his aides listened for any deviation from his original statement. A decade ago it would have felt strange talking about magical islands, telepathy, and talking monsters. But because kaiju sightings had escalated in recent years it no longer felt strange. Instead, it felt strange by the fact that they no longer felt strange. The world was becoming more...dangerous? Not exactly. Unpredictable? Definitely. Exciting? That depended upon one's point of view.

When Shindo recounted what happened on Pangea Island, the prime minister nodded in reflection. No one scoffed.

"No one else was taken with you into the island's interior?"

"No."

"No one else had gone ashore?"

"To my knowledge, no."

The prime minister nodded in satisfaction as he glanced down at the statements made by his friend Yomo, Sayoko and Captain Takagi. Their statements made the same claim. No one other than Shindo had been on the island.

"So we have nothing other than your word to confirm what happened on that island." The prime minister leaned back in his chair and eyed Shindo with a knowing look that he believed that there was more to the tale than what Shindo was willing to disclose, and he was interested to hear what else Shindo had to say.

Shindo expected this hearing to segue into the losses the navy suffered while chasing after a monster that turned out to be no threat at all. He bore that responsibility. He was the one who put the pressure on to hunt down Brown Scale. If he had kept his mouth shut and minded his place, those men who were killed aboard the oiler could still be alive today.

Shindo was ready to take the blame. It was a point of honor and self-respect to accept the consequences rather than take the path of cowards and make excuses.

"Yes, Prime Minister, that is correct," Shindo said. "You only have my word."

"And you have no evidence to offer? No audio or video recordings? No artifacts?"

"Just the mud on my uniform."

"Hm," the prime minister intoned, and smiled. "That was amazing work you did. The Chief of Staff of the Maritime Self Defense Force has a word for you. Admiral Ozeki?"

Admiral Ozeki, the head of the Japanese navy, put on his glasses and read from a sheet of paper that he held in both hands. "The kaiju known as Brown Scale has been involved in the Flock attack on our destroyer, *Sakai-maru*. Fourteen members of her crew had been killed in that attack. Weeks later Brown Scale was involved in the destruction of a smuggler's base. There an estimated seventy-five persons had died as a result of the attack. Later, Brown Scale aided his Flock in the destruction of a United States aircraft carrier, her planes, and escorts. Nearly all hands had been lost. Finally, our task force headed by Captain Takagi, encountered this armored kaiju that had been causing so much destruction and loss of life across the Pacific. In this encounter, instead of attacking the ships of the Japanese Maritime Self Defense Force, it joined forces with our naval personnel against Tiamatodon. Because of Brown Scale's aid, the officers and crew of the task force were able to withdraw from the combat zone with minimum casualties. The only deciding factor the department of the Maritime Self Defense Force can find to account for this change in Brown Scale's behavior in this encounter from the previous three encounters is the presence of Yamaguchi, Shindo, of the Defense Ministry.

"The Japanese Maritime Self Defense Force would like to hereby acknowledge the achievement of Yamaguchi, Shindo. His actions while alone with this kaiju had convinced this creature to not only spare the lives of his countrymen and women but protect them so they may return home safe."

Admiral Ozeki lowered the paper and added, "I forwarded a recommendation that you should be awarded a Medal of Honor. On behalf of the service members of the Maritime Self Defense Force I wish to thank you for your bravery, and your ingenuity."

The admiral led the entire room in giving Shindo an applause.

Shindo opened his mouth in surprise. He leaned close to the mic to make himself heard. "Thank you, but I can hardly…"

Goro motioned to him to hold his tongue.

Shindo decided his chief was right. This was not the time and place to set the record straight. He stopped talking and accepted their thanks.

"Just out of curiosity," the prime minister said to Shindo, "why do you think Brown Scale helped our people escape Tiamtadon?"

"As I said in my report, I think Brown Scale wanted us to get home so we can convince you to leave him alone. That's all he wants. To be left alone."

The prime minister nodded. He was satisfied with the answer.

After the prime minister closed the hearing, he held a number of meetings regarding Pangea Island. Now that there was a new set of witnesses, plus evidence—the mud on Shindo's uniform—to verify the island's existence, the government needed to determine what can and cannot be revealed to the public, to Japan's allies, and the United Nations. The government swore the sailors under Takagi's command to silence until further notice. Eventually someone was going to say something that would be an addition to what will be issued in official records. A strategy needed to be devised to deal with that scenario.

In the meantime, the issue that weighed on Shindo's conscience, the men who lost their lives because of his bad judgment call, was lost in the shuffle, and forgotten.

Goro had Shindo undergo a psychiatric evaluation. No one knew what affect psychic contact with alien entities would have on the human mind.

From what the on-staff psychiatrist could tell, Shindo suffered no serious harm. Just mild depression and anxiety. Overall, his evaluation rated him in satisfactory mental health. Shindo's prior evaluation rated him A-1 fit for duty. Goro gave Shindo three weeks leave. He ordered Shindo to get his mind off things. Turn off the TV. No newspapers. No online social media.

A week into his leave, Goro checked up on him. They had lunch at Dhaba's. It was midafternoon, in between mealtimes. Most of the tables were empty.

"How have you been?" Goro asked. "Getting enough sleep?"

Shindo nodded.

"Any nightmares?"

Shindo grinned. "Nightmares aren't necessarily a symptom of anything."

"Well? Have you been having nightmares?"

Shindo shrugged. "Naw. Nothing much." Nothing that he wanted to worry his chief about. Last night was the fourth time he dreamt that his mother burst into his room and tried to stab him do death. At least this time in the dream he pulled the skin off the specter's face, revealing that it was not his mother trying to kill him but some hag with the complexion of a rotten apple. The dream ended with him blocking the knife with his pillow and knocking the hag out the window with a solid punch to the jaw. Shindo would like to think that was a sign that he was coping.

Goro eyed him for a bit and then let the matter drop.

Up on the TV, NHK News ended their update with a segment on Mushita Electronic's Type VII laser cannon. Anchorwoman Tomoko Mahiko gave the report:

"Called the '*Heartbreaker*', the Type VII laser cannon completed its first trial run this past summer. It was mounted to the *Kaga-maru*, a Maritime Self-Defense Force destroyer, and taken down to the South Pacific, down into Kaiju Country. There it successfully repelled Tylogon, the kaiju *Tylosaurus*. At two hundred meters in length, Tylogon is the largest sea monster on record." A silhouette of Tylogon appeared in the upper right hand corner of the broadcast along with a silhouette of a destroyer for size comparison.

"Kaiju analysts have criticized the achievement by saying navy ships have driven Tylogon away before," Mahiko continued. "However, in this instance, the *Heartbreaker* had cut a deep wound into Tylogon's flesh, something that has not been done before. Sayoko Kuta, head of the research and development department for Mushita Electronics, responded to the criticism by stating that the point is not that her company's new weapon was able to blunt Tylogon's attack. The scale of the injury is the point. The *Heartbreaker* will prove its worth against more aggressive creatures. The Type VII laser cannon could kill the next kaiju that makes landfall on the home islands.

"To a degree, Sayoko's point was validated when the *Kaga-maru* and her escorts encountered Tiamatodon later in their mission. The *Heartbreaker* reportedly stopped Tiamadon's advance on the ships, allowing them to escape with the loss of one vessel.

"Based on these successes, the government has finalized the purchase of twenty Type VIIs and granted additional funds for the development of this promising series of weapons. The total amount is to be settled at a later date."

Tomoko Mahiko thanked the viewers for watching and ended the update.

"Sayoko sure was happy when the defense minister signed the contract," Shindo commented with a side grin.

"You should be happy, too," Goro chided.

"I'm happy."

"No you're not. You're drinking beer. You never drink beer unless you're feeling sorry for yourself."

"Chief, I'm fine."

"Nonsense!" Goro lowered his voice so the wait staff didn't overhear him. "You're upset because you thought the mission was a mistake. It wasn't a mistake. This new Flock kaiju had to be checked out. Pressuring your superiors to go after that beast was the right thing to do. Not that I condone that sort of behavior, but in this case I am glad you did. Too often Tiamatodon blinds us to the fact there are other monsters out there besides him."

Shindo lowered his voice as well when he replied. "What I can't seem to get anyone to understand is that the problem had resolved itself by the time we found Brown Scale. Once he settled on that island he had no intention of leaving. People seem to think I convinced him to save our task force. I didn't convince him of anything."

"Have you ever considered that you might have been the right person in the right place at the right time? Imagine if General Umezo had been there instead of you. After reading his mind, Brown Scale would have probably flown up here and leveled Tokyo!"

Shindo suppressed a laugh.

"When that creature read your mind, it must have seen that you could be trusted, that you were its best hope of being left alone. It protected you so you could return home, so you could tell the world what you had discovered. Now, we know that we can leave that animal alone and it knows that it can leave us alone. Peaceful coexistence between man and beast. This is why everyone else is so happy. You saved lives. Far more than have been lost. It's not obvious, but it's true. Far more have been saved than lost."

Shindo couldn't argue. It was just that up until now the definition of success had been stopping a monster dead in its tracks before it could do more damage. The emergency seemed over by the time he found Brown Scale. But was it really over? What if both sides, human and the brown Flock pterosaur, didn't know they could leave each other alone? There would have been future battles, future deaths, and they would be all for nothing. He had to admit, his chief had a point.

The guilt fell from his shoulders.

"You're right. Something was accomplished." Shindo smiled.

Goro sighed in satisfaction.

"I'm not in the mood for beer anymore." Shindo set the glass away from his place at the table. He called over the waitress and ordered his usual, a mint lassi.

"Since you hadn't touched it, I'll take it." Goro set Shindo's discarded drink next to his. "Never let good beer go to waste!"

When Shindo received his mint lassi, Goro held up his beer. "To you, Shindo. You're star is rising."

"Thank you." Shindo clinked his class with Goro's.

"Kanpai."

The Bestiary

A Guide to the Creatures Populating *I Shall Not Mate*

The Flock

       According to Native American legend, the Thunderbird ruled the skies. It lived on a mountain that floated in the air. Thunder cracked when it flapped its wings. In battle, the Thunderbird rained down lightning bolts upon its enemies and when it was hungry, it swooped down over the sea and grabbed a whale in its talons and then flew back up to its mountain to eat its catch. Could the legend of the Thunderbird have been based on sightings of a giant pterosaur?

On April 26, 1890, the *Tombstone Epitaph* published a story with the headline: *FOUND ON THE DESERT: A Strange Winged Monster Discovered And Killed on the Huachuea Desert.* According to the story, two ranchers shot and killed an animal that resembled "a huge alligator with an extremely elongated tail and an immense pair of wings." Upon examination, they found that the creature had no feathers and the wings were made of a thin membrane. Could this creature have been a pterosaur?

In 1943, Allied radar operators stationed in Salamaua, New Guinea, spotted an object circling the coast. The object "systematically dropped below radar range while over the water, popped back up and continue its circle." Despite an oncoming storm, P-38s under the command of 2nd Lt. Arthur Daniels were dispatched from the Wau airfield to investigate the object. By the time Daniels' planes had arrived, the object flew inland at "a speed that was too swift for the radar to track."

At the same time Satoshi Hideki of the First Sentai was escorting a squadron of Ki-21 "Sally" bombers. Their mission was to destroy the Wau airfield. By then the storm was in full force. The heavy rains sluiced down Satoshi's canopy. His Kawasaki fighter bucked in the winds. "It was crazy being up there in the air," Satoshi recalled. "It was like trying to see through a thick, gray syrup." But that was the point. By being crazier than the Allies, Satoshi's superiors hoped that the foul weather would ground Allied interceptors and thereby allow the Japanese to complete their sortie with impunity.

As luck would have it, Daniels' fighters returned to base just as the Japanese bombers with their fighter escort came skirting around the mountains. A dogfight in torrential rain ensued. Seven of the twelve bombers survived long enough to drop their bombs. Fireballs erupted out of the jungle. It was impossible to tell if the target had been hit. Satoshi shot down two enemy planes before becoming separated from his squadron. He returned to base, alone.

On the way back, the storm cleared. The sun shined through the clouds like rays of hope. Yet, Satoshi felt ill at ease, as if he were being watched.

His suspicions were confirmed when he glimpsed an aircraft as it flew underneath his plane. The unidentified craft did not swing back into view nor fire a shot. Hideki hoped it had crashed in the jungle below but his nerves were on edge. He still felt as though there was an oppressive presence watching him.

Then the aircraft returned. Hideki could see that he was mistaken. His pursuer was not an airplane but a great white bird. It had scales on its face and an enormous sail atop its head. It gave him an admonishing look as if to say, "You shouldn't be up here. It's dangerous."

The great bird flew alongside him until he reached the coast. It then veered away and flew toward the mountains. Satoshi no longer felt the oppressive presence. In his report he stated that he did not feel that the great white bird was the cause of his unease. Something else was out there and he believed the bird was protecting him from it. Was the great white bird a pterosaur? What did the radar operators detect flying over the coast? Was it a pterosaur? Arthur Daniels saw nothing unusual on his flight. Both Satoshi and the radar operator reports were chalked up as Foo fighter sightings and forgotten.

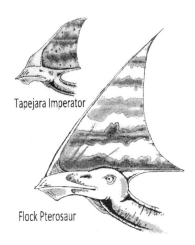

Tapejara Imperator

Flock Pterosaur

It was not until 1952 when the fact that pterosaurs lived among us became undeniable. About thirty pterosaurs attacked vacationers on Bain Lot Beach on the island of Tahiti. They ranged in size from an adult human to an elephant. The creatures killed sixty-nine people and injured over a hundred others. As abruptly as they came, they took to the air, leaving the sun-warmed sands stained with blood. They joined much larger pterosaurs which were circling in the air several miles away. A decade later, a survivor from the massacre, a Californian by the name of Susan Hayworth, experienced a traumatic flashback after viewing Hitchcock's film *The Birds*. She rushed out of the theater, sobbing, "It was just like that! It was just like! Oh God, it was just like that!"

To this day these pterosaurs have been attacking the coasts throughout the Pacific. The pterosaurs have been described as being white in color with pink wingtips. They have scales on their faces and limbs and fur on their torsos. The sail atop their heads makes them readily recognizable from other flying kaiju. Because they attack en masse, they have been dubbed The Flock. Coincidentally, the white pterosaurs identify themselves in their own language of clucks and hisses as "The Flock".

Biology

The Flock are the direct descendants of the *Tapejara*, specifically *Tapejara Imperator*. However, the nomenclature for this topic can be confusing because depending upon the source, *Tapejara Imperator* is also known as *Tupandactylus Imperator*. Those sources will go on to say that *Tupandactylus* is a different species from the *Tapejara*. In any case, the *Tapejara* and *Tupandactylus* fall under the *Tapejara* family. Thus the Flock can be recognized as a *Tapejara*.

The fossils for *T. Imperator* have been found in the Early Cretaceous Crato Formation in Brazil's Araripe Basin. The pterosaur has a distinctive toucan-shaped beak and an enormous head crest. The crest is framed by two prongs, one which extends from the back of the head and another which rises up from the tip of the beak and sweeps over the top of the head in a wide arch.

The Flock have a similar arrangement except the prong extending from the beak is articulated so it can be folded down while not in use. This articulation allows the creature to lower its sail while in flight and turn its head without changing its course.

The keels on the breastbones for pterosaurs tend to be smaller than those of birds. The muscles to the wings are attached to the breastbone's keel. The smaller

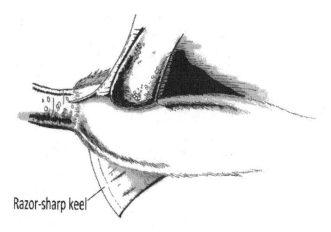

Razor-sharp keel

the keel, the smaller the wing muscles. Among the Flock, the opposite is true. They have enormous keels in proportion to other flying animals, so much so the keels stick out of the chest. A sheath of keratin covers the exposed bone, giving it a razor's edge. The Flock use this exposed bone like a hatchet, ramming it into enemies as they buzz over their enemy's head. Witnesses have seen the keels crack the skulls of opposing kaiju.

As stated earlier, keel size impacts the size of the wing muscles. This holds true for the Flock. Because of the ample amount of surface area for muscle attachment, the Flock have proportionally the largest wing muscles among pterosaurs and are among the most powerful flyers on Earth. They have been tracked at speeds falling just short of Mach One. Adult members can glide across the Pacific and fly half way around the world without tiring.

Despite these impressive characteristics, the Flock are often the prey of other kaiju. Most adults are around fifty meters in height with a few reaching sixty-five meters. Compare that to Super Allosaurus, who is seventy meters tall, two hundred meters long, and ten times heavier. Because the Flock needs to be lightweight in order to fly, their hide is not as thick as other kaiju, which leaves them vulnerable to human weapons.

Flock hatchlings are about a meter and a half to two meters in height at birth. They experience a growth spurt in their third month, gaining ten meters in height each week. This spurt lasts for about four weeks. At the end of the fourth week they reach adult height, which is fifty meters. They continue to grow, albeit at a much slower rate, until death.

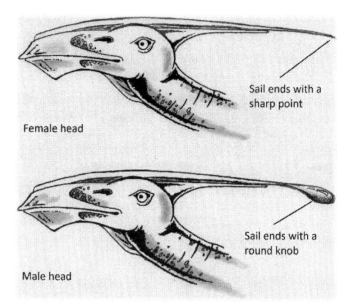

Female head

Sail ends with a
sharp point

Male head

Sail ends with a
round knob

Wing growth varies depending upon the size of the clutch. Hatchlings from small clutches (one to three eggs) are able to fly within days of birth while hatchlings from large clutches (four or more eggs) wait several weeks before their wings are strong enough for flight. The reason for this is unknown. Some scientists guess that there is a survival mechanism at work. After disease and predation takes its toll, a hatchling or two from a large clutch will survive long enough to become adults while a small clutch stands a high risk of not having any survivors at all. Thus the hatchlings from small clutches enjoy a faster wing growth, which then gives them parity in their chances for survival with the larger clutches.

As a counterbalance to their vulnerability, nature provided the Flock with a keen intelligence. The intellect of a single Flock pterosaur is equal to that of a dolphin. As the number of pterosaurs in a Flock increases, their intelligence increases. However, it must be noted the members of a Flock must be within close proximity of each other or else their intellect decreases back to its original baseline of that of a dolphin.

When they do stick close together and continue to breed, their intelligence increases to the point where the Flock exhibits psychic abilities. Hence it has been a priority for the nations of the world to destroy their nesting grounds. No one knows what limit the Flock can reach, if there is even a limit. We can be grateful that in the contest for survival, nature had maintained a balance by making the Flock physically inferior, otherwise if the Flock were as durable as the other kaiju, the Flock would undoubtedly take over the Earth.

Vital Statistics
Offspring
Height: 1.5 meters
Wingspan: 3 meters
Weight: 70 pounds

Juveniles
Height: 2-50 meters
Wingspan: 5-140 meters
Weight: 110 pounds –4,000 tons

Adults
Height: 50-65 meters
Wingspan: 140-145 meters
Weight: 4,000 tons – 5,000 tons

Armor: None
Weapons: Razor sharp chest keel
Special Abilities: Keen intelligence*, Psychic Abilities*

*These abilities are dependent upon the number of Flock members in a given area.

Tylogon

Keisuke Adachi expected October 24, 1962, to be no different from any other day out on the high seas. He was a harpoon gunner on the Japanese whaling vessel, *Hikeda maru*. The spotter sighted their first quarry of the season, a female minke whale. Keisuke took aim at the minke and scored a hit, killing the animal on the first shot. As his shipmates prepared to reel in their catch a massive gray-green creature broke the surface. It grabbed their whale in its jaws and dove back into the sea. The waves from its wake crashed into the ship, causing it to bob like a toy in a bath tub.

The incident put the whalers in a state of shock. Once the captain gathered his senses, he ordered his men to get back to work. They still had to make a living.

They tracked down a second pod of minke whales. The spotter singled out an elderly male, a big one—ten meters in length—trailing behind its companions. The *Hikeda* closed within firing range. Keisuke scored another hit. One shot. One kill. As they were about to power up the winches, the sea monster grabbed their catch again. This time the harpoon cable did not snap right away. The ship was pulled forward with a jolt. Keisuke saved himself from being thrown overboard by clinging to his cannon, but his assistants were not so lucky. They rolled off the bow and into the thrashing waves.

After Keisuke's friends were pulled back on board, the captain ordered the crew to set sail in hopes of finding a pod that was not in the sea monster's hunting grounds, but the spotter sighted the monster following them. It was clear to the whalers that all they were doing was providing free meals for this kaiju.

Keisuke described the creature as a gigantic whale. "I didn't see much of it. Just a glimpse of the head and part of the back when it dove into the water. I'd say it was fifty meters long. And its teeth were bigger than an Orca's. Largest I've seen in a whale. They were like a crocodile's."

Professor Kiyoshi Shimura, a paleontologist from Tokyo University, caused a sensation when he identified the animal as a *Basilosaurus*, an extinct whale that lived during the Eocene. Cryptozoologists fanned out across the Pacific to verify the existence of Keisuke's whale. The fact that his whale was twice the length of any *Basilosaurus* found in the fossil record only seasoned everyone's excitement.

It took six years before anyone found Keisuke's whale, and the seamen who encountered the beast were not even looking for it. The beast burst from the water and slapped the crates from the deck of a containership that was midway in its trip to Los Angeles. It swam away with a yellow, forty foot long container in its jaws. The crew could not see much other than the bright yellow box. The sea beast was swimming too fast and "and kicking up quite a spray" of water. It dove from sight about a hundred sixty meters from the ship.

From the way the crates were disheveled at the back of the ship, it looked as though a giant hand had slapped them, but how was the captain going to prove to the port authorities that a monster had attacked the ship?

While he fretted, the box the sea beast had stolen surfaced on the starboard side of the ship, fifteen meters away. In the next breath the beast leapt out of the water and belly-flopped atop the ship. The sea monster lay splayed across the entire length of the ship with its flippers hanging over the sides. Its smooth scales were slick and shiny with sea water.

A Taiwanese freighter caught up with the stricken vessel. "It was a miracle the container ship was still afloat," a sailor recalled. "The deck couldn't have been more than a meter above the water. The monster made no attempt to attack us. He just watched us as we watched him. He roared once, as if to say hello. Luckily, some of the crew were close enough for us to rescue them. They were clinging to the containers that were floating in the water, but we didn't dare send anyone out to the other ship. There was no telling what the monster might do. Our captain tried to radio the ship and got no response. All we could do was sail on while the sea monster laid its head on the bow and closed its eyes. It was as if it were sunning itself."

The crew of the Taiwanese freighter snapped the first photographs. Its existence now documented, Keisuke's whale turned out to be four times the length Keisuke had estimated—200 meters.

Biology

The photographs taken by the crew of the Taiwanese cargo ship showed that the sea beast was not a *Basilosaurus*, but a *Tylosaurus*, which was a marine lizard that had gone extinct with the dinosaurs at the end of the Mesozoic. The Japanese press dubbed the monster "Tylogon" which is a name that has stuck since it was first published in the newspapers in 1968.

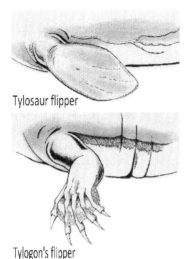

Tylosaur flipper

Tylogon's flipper

Scientists have speculated whether or not Tylogon is an accurate representation of what tylosaurs were like in terms of color, scale texture, body proportions and so forth. Paleo artists have featured tylosaurs with a fin running along their back. Tylogon sports a fin along his back similar to what artists have rendered with one additional feature. The fin is supported by sharp spines. The sharpness of those spines have caused scientists to wonder if they were meant to provide protection. If so, protection from what? Tylogon is the largest known predator in the sea. The fact that the spines are sharp could indicate that even larger marine predators exist.

On the other hand, the spines could have protected the creature when it was young. But that raises another question. Who were Tylogon's parents? Is he the only one?

Thus far only one tylogon creature has been seen at a time. It could mean there are few tylogons. Or there are many but they live near the ocean floor, coming up to the surface on rare occasion.

In any case, Tylogon shows evidence that his species is evolving. His limbs are in an intermediary stage between being a flipper and a paw. The bones in the flippers are larger than those of his tylosaur ancestors and are articulated like fingers, and they are tipped with claws. If there are other tylogons, in a few million years Tylogon's descendants could become terrestrial creatures.

Tylogon is dark gray in color with a hint of green. His underbelly is a bright cream color. He is a rotund creature, which often misleads people in mistaking him for an enormous whale. His scales are smooth as a marine mammal's, although his skin has a pebbly texture around the face and neck. He has a row of short, conical spikes jutting out from either side of his snout, which serves as a display feature designating him as a male. They also help deter his kaiju opponents from trying to bite down on his head.

He free ranges across the entire Pacific, including the artic regions. Tylgon has been blamed for ship sinkings in the North Atlantic and Mediterranean, however the eye witnesses have described creatures that don't quite fit Tylogon's appearance, so investigators are not convinced he has prowled any waters other than the Pacific.

As an apex predator, Tylogon has no fear of being killed. He has a devil-may-care attitude. In his own way he likes everyone around him and if you served as a tasty meal for him he likes you that much more, and will remember you fondly. Unlike other kaiju he does not engage in wanton destruction, but he does like to play. However, he plays rough. His horseplay often results in loss of life.

Vital Statistics
Length: 200 meters
Height (at shoulder): 55 meters
Weight: 70,000 tons

Armor: None
Weapons: Can spew stomach acid, has an electrified bite, claws on his flippers
Special abilities: Aquatic

Tiamatodon, the Two-Headed One

Tiamatodon is feared by man and animal alike. Day and night, year after year without ceasing, Tiamatodon seeks out living creatures to kill. Large or small. It does not matter. The kaiju has razed entire cities. To date, no weapon has been able to penetrate its tough hide. The only saving grace is the fact the world is a big place and Tiamatodon is sluggish on foot and it rarely returns to the places it has already left its mark.

Tiamatodon is a mutant. It is aware of this fact and that it should have been born as two separate megalosaurs, a male and female. Instead the brother is now a Siamese twin with his sister. They resent what had been done to them and are envious of the normal animals in the animal kingdom. This resentment has boiled over into hatred. Hatred is what has turned Tiamatodon into an engine of destruction.

Background

The story of Tiamatodon begins with the atomic tests of the 1950s. The US military discovered prehistoric life on three Micronesian Islands in the Pacific Proving Grounds. The animals were identical to those that lived during the mid-Jurassic Period, including dinosaurs. Examples include stegosaurs, such as *Huayangosaurus* and *Lexovisaurus*, sauropods such as *Shunosaurus* and *Cetiosaurus*, although only a single herd of cetiosaurs have been observed on one of the three islands, ornithopods such as *Xiaosaurus*, and finally giant carnivores such as the *Megalosaurus*. The islands were named Batho, after the Bathonian age, Bajo, after the Bajocian age, and Callo, after the Callovian age. All three ages make up the middle years of the Jurassic.

The United States Atomic Energy Commission found that the flora and fauna had been unaffected by the atomic tests even though radioactivity readings of the islands showed dangerous levels of radiation. In 1958, a team of researchers, without authorization from the AEC, subjected specimens from Bajo Island to radioactivity to see how much they could absorb. Several *Megalosaurus* eggs were included in the studies. What the scientists did not know was that one of the eggs had a double yolk. The radiation fused the yolks and out hatched a Siamese twin with no arms.

The Siamese twin escaped from its pen. At the time Tiamatodon was about the size of an adult human. The researchers were unable to find it and concluded it had become prey to another carnivore.

Three years later, the International Whaling Commission issued a report that an entire pod of Humpback Whales had been found dead. The report described the whales as being "massacred". "Their mutilated corpses left a trail of blood that was a mile long." "Teeth marks had been found on many of the animals." The copy of the report that was released to the public claimed the teeth marks had been caused by sharks, although no sharks had been reported in the area or any other scavengers. It was as if all animal life in the sea avoided the area as though it were cursed.

Whalers had been blamed for the massacre and since the dead whales had been found floating eight miles from the Kurile Islands, the fingers were pointed at Japan and the Soviet Union. The Soviets and the Japanese denied responsibility. Japanese intelligence agents obtained an original copy of the report which contained information that had been redacted under the advisement of the United Nations Security Council. Japan brought this report to the world's attention at the UN. The redacted material included the following: The bite marks did not match any known shark. Also, the bite marks were the cause of death for only several of the whales. Most of them had been killed by "a beam of intense heat". No whaling vessel utilized a heat ray. The United Nations Security Council had hoped to find and eradicate this beast before it could cause a panic which would then lead to a negative impact on commercial shipping across the Pacific. But the truth was out. Japan was vindicated and the UN was stuck with a cover-up scandal. Whether the international community wanted to admit it or not, the whales had been killed by a new kaiju that had yet to be seen or identified.

Two months later the culprit revealed itself. A sole survivor from a sunken freighter claimed that a two-headed dinosaur rose up out of the waters and spewed "purple fire" from its mouths. The fire destroyed the ship. As the ship sank, the dinosaur turned its fire upon the sailors who were trying to escape in the life boats. No sooner did his story hit the headlines, the two-headed dinosaur made landfall in New Zealand, wiping out a coastal town. This time the kaiju was captured on film, which helped the scientific community to confirm the creature's identity. It was the Siamese-twin megalosaur that had escaped its pen on Bajo Island, except now it was sixty-five meters tall.

The current state of the crisis

Tokyo University's star paleontologist, Professor Kiyoshi Shimura, christened the creature Tiamatodon after Tiamat, the Babylonian goddess of chaos and destruction. The name is apt. Since the 1960s, Tiamatodon has grown to 120 meters in height. It can summon storms and draw lightning from those storms to fuel the plasma energy it fires out of its two mouths. Where these powers came from, no one knows. It did not breathe fire while it was a subject of study on Bajo Island. Many fear that the creature will gain new powers as it continues to grow, and since it is a mutant, no one can say how much larger it will get. It may never stop growing.

The navies of the Pacific maintain a watch for the beast. Once Tiamatodon is spotted, evacuation orders are issued to communities that are at risk of being attacked. Ships are rerouted to avoid contact. Thus far, mankind has learned to live with this beast, but behind the scenes, scientists and engineers are working tirelessly to design a weapon that will end Tiamatodon's reign of terror.

Vital Statistics
Length: 150 meters
Height: 120 meters
Weight: 65,000 tons

Armor: Thick hide, impervious to most weapons
Weapons: fires plasma beams from the mouth
Special abilities: Psychic, summons storms and draws energy from the sky in the form of lightning. The energy powers its plasma beams.

About the Author

Neil Riebe has been a lifelong fan of Japanese giant monsters since seeing *King Kong vs Godzilla* back in the 70s. The three-part story *Godzilla vs Atragon*, which was published in *G-Fan* issues #9 through #11, inspired him to write his multi-part Godzilla stories. These stories included *Godzilla vs Super Allosaurus*, which saw print in *G-Fan* issues #15 through #17, *Battle of Manazura Island*, published in *G-Fan* #25, and *Rodana*, published in *G-Fan* #42. After Toho asked *G-Fan* to cease publishing fan fiction based on their characters, Neil posted subsequent stories on Fan Fiction.net. While writing kaiju fan fiction, he also wrote an article for *Japanese Giants* #10 and the forewords to *Gfantis vs Guest Monsters* anthology and John LeMay's *The Big Book of Japanese Giant Monster Movies Vol. 1: 1954-1982*. Matt Dennion, author of the popular *Atomic Rex* novels, invited Neil to contribute a short story to his *Attack of the Kaiju* anthology. Since then Neil has switched from kaiju fan fiction to writing original kaiju stories. He has another story awaiting release in *Attack of the Kaiju Volume 2*. *I Shall Not Mate* is his first kaiju novel.

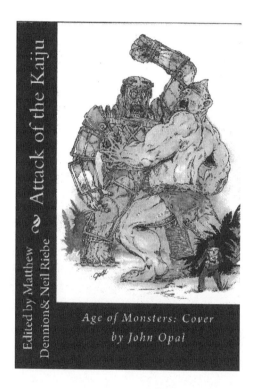

Also available

Lost no longer. You heard the rumors. Now get the facts. Read about the kaiju projects that nearly reached the silver screen, the alternate storylines for popular Godzilla movies, and obscure science fiction films produced by the Japanese film industry.

"Great fun and tons of revelations!"—Mike Bogue, author of Apocalypse Then: American and Japanese Atomic Cinema, 1951-1967

"As close as I have felt to being that kid in the movie store again."—Colin McMahon, ATTACK! of the B-Movie Monsters

Available in print or Kindle Edition on Amazon.com

Available soon

Do you hear that roar? Do you feel the ground shake? It's time to duck back into the shelters. The kaiju are back!

Attack of the Kaiju Volume 2

Many of the authors who had made volume 1 epic have returned—Matt Dennion (*Atomic Rex*), Christofer Nigro (*Megadrak, Beast of the Apocalypse*), Zach Cole (*Titans Unleashed*), and Neil Riebe (*I Shall Not Mate*), along with names who are new to the series—Christopher Conde and Michael Eads. To be released from Wild Hunt Press.

Made in the USA
Monee, IL
18 May 2020